BRAINBENDER

BOOK 9 OF THE *SPIES LIE* SERIES

DS KANE
(dskane@dskane.com)

ISBN: 978-0-9996554-4-3 (paperback)
ISBN: 978-0-9996554-2-9 (Kindle)
ISBN: 978-0-9996554-3-6 (ePub)

Cover design by Jeroen Ten Berge
[www.jeroentenberge.com]

Print and ebook layout by eBooks By Barb
for booknook.biz

Praise for DS Kane's *Spies Lie* Series

Bloodridge

"A globe-trotting spy thriller dense with intriguing insider's knowledge."—*Kirkus Reviews*

"I thoroughly enjoyed this book... It is definitely a page-turner."—*Judge, 22nd Annual Writer's Digest Self-Published Book Awards*

"This is a sizzler torn straight from tomorrow's headlines. *Bloodridge* by D.S. Kane is one you won't want to miss." —*John Reinhard Dizon, author of* **Nightcrawler** *and* **Wolf Man**

"What a wild ride! Filled with adventure and suspense and kept me on the edge of my seat. There wasn't a slow moment in it. Reminiscent of Ludlum and Follett." — *Sharon Law Tucker, author of* **How to Be a BadAss: A Survival Guide for Women**

DeathByte

"Readers who adore action-packed thrillers in the vein of Robert Ludlum's Bourne series will enjoy its many double-crossings."—*Kirkus Reviews*

"This was a great thriller... and the speed of the plot was breathtaking."—*Judge, 22nd Annual Writer's Digest Self-Published Book Awards*

Swiftshadow

"A must read for lovers of this genre." —*Sheri A. Wilkinson, book blogger*

"The high stakes and dizzily paced action will hook genre fans from the first page."—*Kirkus Reviews*

GrayNet

"Conspiracy theorists are sure to devour this novel."
—*Mallory Heart Reviews*

"Nonstop action and suspense starring the definition of a strong female lead."—*Kirkus Reviews*

Baksheesh (Bribes)

"More wild, violent adventures in the world of international espionage."—*Kirkus Reviews*

"This Story Should be an Audible Selection... Could be a Major Motion Picture..."—*Charles W, TOP 500 REVIEWER*

ProxyWar

"The latest adventure in a series that only grows more engaging with each installment."—*Kirkus Reviews*

"Mr. Kane saved the best for last of course he left open the next installment. And he brought back accidental spy Jon Sommers to finish things up. Please write fast Mr Kane so we can see what happens next!" —*Richard L. Cooper, Amazon Reviewer*

CypherGhost

"After working as a covert operative for over a decade and travelling the globe, DS Kane now writes fictions about how intelligence agencies craft lies to sway and manipulate their national policy. His latest techno-thriller CypherGhost is a fast-paced and gripping story which will keep you up reading the whole night. DS Kane, without a doubt, is a great story-teller. When we picked up the latest installment of Kane's Spies Lies series, we got hooked from the beginning. The author does a wonderful job of fictionalizing the crossroads of politics, technology and national security in an entertaining plot.

The book is written is a very easy language and can be read in one sitting. Although we can categorize this novel as a thriller, the author has toyed to some extent with some science fiction themes which make the story more absorbing. Overall, a highly recommended read for the lovers of popular thrillers."—*Mystery Tribune*

"Packed with enough terrifying detail to feel at least moderately plausible, if not horrifyingly prescient."
—*Kirkus Reviews*

"If you are into spy novels then look no further. The 7th book in the Spies Lie series is every bit as good as the 6 that preceded it. D.S. Kane is the pseudonym of a former CIA covert operative who clearly knows what he is talking about. Characters are well developed and plots are exciting and not far removed from what the operations of a modern intelligence agency might get up to. Do yourself a huge favour and read the book, you won't be disappointed... then once you have finished that you have 6 other books in the series that you need to get your hands on as soon as possible! Other books in the series are as follows 1. Bloodridge, 2. DeathByte, 3. Swiftshadow, 4. GrayNet, 5. Baksheesh, 6. ProxyWar. They are all available from Amazon. Do yourself a huge favour and read them now!" —*N G McKenzie*

MindField

"In the eighth installment of Kane's (CypherGhost, 2016, etc.) Spies Lie series, a hacker and her parents aim to uncover the truth about a CIA conspiracy.

A fast-paced thriller with an empowered young female protagonist. —*Kirkus Reviews*

BOOKS IN THE *SPIES LIE* SERIES

Bloodridge, Book 1
(http://www.amazon.com/dp/B00K0029J0)

DeathByte, Book 2
(http://www.amazon.com/dp/B00L2LLKSC)

Swiftshadow, Book 3
(http://www.amazon.com/dp/B00MJ5KXKG)

GrayNet, Book 4
(http://www.amazon.com/dp/B00P8HRT9U)

Baksheesh (Bribes), Book 5
(http://www.amazon.com/dp/B010NR3RD6)

ProxyWar, Book 6
(http://www.amazon.com/dp/B018YS91CM)

CypherGhost, Book 7
(http://www.amazon.com/dp/B01MTPXRZ5)

MindField, Book 8
(https://www.amazon.com/dp/B077X44RR9)

And now, **brAInbender**... with more to come.

For my spouse, Andrea Brown,
who has made my life an incredible adventure.

Contents

PART 1

PART 2

PART 3

PART 4

Disclaimer

This is a work of fiction. All of the characters and events depicted here are the work of the author's mind. Most but not all of the places are real.

PART 1

PART 1

CHAPTER 1

51st Floor, Strumler Tower Capital Hotel, Washington, DC

November 21, 2:09 p.m.

United States president-elect Daniel Strumler ate a toasted-cheese sandwich overstuffed with heirloom tomatoes while he watched the afternoon news. A Fox News commentator said that the new Israeli ambassador to the United Nations was speaking about Strumler. During the presidential campaign, Strumler had told his supporters that he would rather develop jobs in America than ship arms to defend Israel. He feared this speech might be a vehicle for Israel's payback.

He immediately changed the channel to watch the speech.

The man addressing the General Assembly dwarfed the two Israeli bodyguards at the edges of the stage. He was huge and his uniform couldn't hide his muscles. But, thought Strumler, *this man isn't the Israeli UN Ambassador*. He'd been told the ambassador was a woman. And, since when did a diplomat wear a military uniform? Strumler examined the man's face and decided that the man seemed too young to be seasoned. *I wonder if this new ambassador is former Mossad?*

He turned up the volume.

"...for you today. First, I have urgent information concerning a set of messages Israel intercepted about an impending attempt to assassinate the president-elect of the United States. We discovered this intelligence threat while we were tracking Russian communications. As a result, I also have evidence to present. Convincing evidence. We believe the American president-elect is compromised by the Russians and that they want to keep him from being arrested and tried as a traitor. Moving to the first of these items, here is the evidence..."

As Strumler watched the "ambassador" speak, his rage turned to acid in his throat. He grabbed his ever-present bottle of antacid tablets and popped them into his mouth, one after another.

The television screen finally displayed the name of the speaker: "Israeli Acting Ambassador, Avram Shimmel." The huge man continued speaking and Strumler stood riveted in place, facing the screen. He watched the screen change to display documents he had no idea existed. He listened to tapes of him and a man Shimmel described as "the president-elect's Russian handler," conversations he couldn't even remember having. At first he felt confused. But the threat roused him back into a fit of anger. He rose and began throwing things around the room. Vases, lamps and even the remains of the toasted-cheese sandwich and the plate it was delivered on—all went flying through the air.

Secret Service and Strumler's private bodyguards crashed through the door in response to the commotion. "Sorry, sir," said one of the Secret Service agents. "We heard noise. We thought it might be some threat."

"Leave me be!" Strumler's eyes were nearly popping out of his head.

* * *

Ann Sashakovich reached the UN Secretariat Building and waited in its lobby for Avram Shimmel to return her call.

She paced the lobby of the tall tower, her notebook computer on, a hacking page reflecting the program's results. Her notebook buzzed. She examined the screen and saw the backtrace she'd initiated while waiting for a taxi at JFK. The backtrace covered all telephone calls originating from or received by the cellphone or landline of Nikolai Puchenko, a Russian FSB officer. Since her first attempt at reading his messages from the Kremlin, Ann had downloaded and installed a Russian-to-English translator app onto her notebook. The backtrace had intercepted a new message from Puchenko's voicemail. She read the text:

> Puchenko, it's your boss. Your ultimate boss. I have decided to send a small assassination team to terminate the existence of your American puppy. Do not have any further contact with the president-elect. The team should be arriving in Washington any time now. I decided not to tell you until after they arrived and were on the ground. Don't worry. I'll not punish you for your own failure.

Ann realized her vision of the events now in progress was incorrect. *Damn! I'm in the wrong city!* She exited the building and ran toward the street to flag a taxi.

On the sidewalk in front of her, she saw a throng of people surrounding a very tall man. It was Avram! She scooted through the people flinging questions at Avram. When she was face-to-face with him, Ann yelled "Avram!"

He stopped and faced her. "Ann, what are you doing here?"

"I left you a voicemail. Didn't—"

"I was speaking before the General Assembly."

The throng of reporters remained silent, focusing on the exchange between the two.

Ann closed the distance so the reporters would have difficulty hearing their conversation. "I'm on my way to Washington, DC. Listen to the message. Decide how you want to handle the problem. I'm sure you'll do the right thing. And, don't worry, I'll tell Cassie and Lee." She backed away and headed to the curbside where she flagged down a taxi and bounced into the back seat. "JFK, any domestic terminal."

The cab rocketed up First Avenue toward the 59th Street Bridge.

While the taxi driver drove Ann down the Brooklyn–Queens Expressway, she called her parents. The call dropped into Cassie's voicemail. "It's Ann. I'm headed toward JFK to take a flight to DC. You guys all need to be there, too. A team of Russian assassins is on its way to Strumler's Washington hotel to kill him. We need to save him so he can be tried for treason. Get yourselves from the United Nations to Strumler's hotel in DC. Call me back when you're en route."

She could see the terminals of JFK flashing by outside the cab's windows. She packed away her phone and notebook. When the cab stopped, she tossed a Franklin to the driver and bolted from the cab.

Inside the terminal, Ann approached a check-in desk and waited her turn in line. "Hi. I just received word that my mama had a heart attack. I have to get to Washington, DC, as soon as I can. Please sell me a ticket on the next available flight."

She offered her credit card, grabbed the boarding pass, and hurried to the TSA Pre-Check security gate.

As she passed through security and trotted toward the departure gate, her cell buzzed. Ann stopped and pulled her cell from her pocket. She examined the screen while she ran. "Mom! Where are you and dad?"

"We're in New York. We got your message. We also got a message from Avram. We'll be meeting up at the private air terminal at JFK. He was able to muster fifty of the two hundred paramilitary he commands in New York at the United Nations. We also have Jon with us. Avram has a Cessna about to take off. Look, Ann, I'm not comfortable with your engaging in a military operation. Go home to Stanford and your studies."

"No way, mom. I'm the best hacker you have available and I can help by telling you where the assassins are located in real time. Remember, I can hack them without a computer. I can use the Bug-Loks the CypherGhost fed me. So use me! I promise I'll stay out of the line of fire."

"Ann, no. Avram called the Secret Service and they're coordinating the op together. You aren't needed. Let the professionals handle this."

Ann thought about her vision of pending events. It had re-formed, accommodating the new set of facts that had emerged. She was sure this new ability would stay with her. "If I'm close enough, I think I may be able to envision their conversations. Don't know how it happened, but I'll know where the assassins are. You need me."

She heard Cassie and Lee talking softly in the background. "Okay. But you'll take orders from Lee and me. You agree?"

Ann smiled. "Yes!"

"We'll meet you inside the Strumler Tower lobby."

She had become a member of the paramilitary team.

* * *

After Ann's flight landed, she took a taxi to the Strumler Tower. Seeing the group of nearly two hundred mercenaries streaming up the stairwells of the building, Ann cast a questioning look at Avram. He said, "These are my UN Paramilitary Force, here courtesy of the local police, the FBI, and the Secret Service. I arranged it all during the flight."

Avram deployed Cassie, Lee, the mercenaries, and himself into strategic locations within the building.

Cassie ordered Ann to sit in the stairwell on the forty-ninth floor, out of harm's way.

Ann found no further trace of the assassination team. It made sense that the team would go dark before their op, so she was sure they had already assumed their positions somewhere within the hotel.

She constantly monitored the security feeds throughout the hotel from her position two floors below Strumler's suite on the fifty-first floor. Half of Avram's paramilitary force was scattered through the hotel's fire stairways. The other half were hidden within the four stairwells leading up to Strumler's suite. Jon was with that group. Cassie and Lee were at Avram's command station in the hotel's delivery platform behind the lobby.

All they could do now was wait.

* * *

Five hours ago, Victor Kreslin and his Russian assassin squad arrived at Strumler Tower. One of his team pointed to a pizza-delivery truck near the side entrance to the building and his second, Igor Nelovich, nodded. Nelovich mugged the pizza-delivery worker in the truck and stole his hat and a pizza in a box.

Then they all rushed twenty floors up the staircase and the "pizza delivery man" knocked on a door in one of the hotel suites. When its occupant said he hadn't ordered any pizza, the "delivery man" told the occupant, "Could be a mistake but the pizza is getting cold. You might as well accept the delivery."

The occupant opened the door.

Kreslin pointed his silenced handgun at the room's two occupants, who both appeared to be tourists. They both held their hands high in the air, but Kreslin shot them each in the head.

The team entered and closed the door behind them.

Sitting in the hotel room, Kreslin and Nelovich reviewed the plan as they waited for the cover of nightfall.

* * *

Kreslin stood by the window, watching the sun descend. "Use the restroom and then eat a slice of the pizza. Once we leave this room at dusk, we can expect things may have changed since we constructed our battle plan. So, be prepared to adjust."

The other seven Russians each nodded, then lined up to use the room's single bathroom.

* * *

Ann's notebook computer buzzed. She examined the screen and sent a text out. All her texts were addressed to Cassie, Lee, Avram, and Jon Sommers:

Russians moving up SW stairwell. Now on 41.

Now she had a fix on where they were. She closed her eyes, and her brain's connection to the hotel network's security cams in the stairs enabled her to watch them climb the stairs. She texted a revision:

They're still heading up the SW staircase. Now at 44. Eight in total. One with a Dragunov sniper rifle. Others armed with semiautomatic handguns.

Although she'd agreed to stay out of combat, Ann's feet moved her, unbidden, to the hallway outside the southwest stairwell on the fiftieth floor. She sought cover at a spot where the hallway turned a corner.

She continued monitoring the security cams. She could hear shots now. At first, single shots, with seconds between each report. Then the shots were more continuous and louder. The Russians were getting closer to her position.

She heard the stairwell door closest to her spring open. She backed away, down the hall, fear chilling her.

Ann shivered as she heard running footsteps coming in her direction. Someone turned the corner of the hallway and came trotting toward her as she backed away. Suddenly, she saw an armed man wearing a mask and holding a handgun. He stood thirty feet away from her now, aiming the pistol at her head.

She was frozen where she stood.

Ann was unarmed. But, she could use her ability to shoot fire from her fingers to save her. He was still too far away for a dead-on headshot at her. Unfortunately for Ann, she was also too far away for her own magic to work.

She placed her notebook computer on the floor and concentrated on her fingers. But, her fingertips were blue. She frowned and held her empty hands in front of her while she waited for the armed man to close the distance.

When he was less than ten feet away and still coming toward her, she thought, *FIRE!* But, she could only smell her fear. Her hands remained ice-cold. Nothing happened.

The Russian moved a step closer and took aim. She guessed she was less than five feet away. Now he had her close enough for a headshot. There was no way he could miss. She thought, *I should have listened to Cassie.* Ann closed her eyes. She couldn't face her own death.

But then she heard the stairwell door open again. She opened her eyes and saw Jon Sommers turn the corner, running toward her. Jon held a handgun and aimed it at the Russian. The Russian reacted to the footsteps approaching him from behind. He whirled around and took aim at Jon.

Her fear converted fast into rage at the Russian. Her fingertips turned from blue to a glowing orange. She aimed her hands at the back of the Russian's head and once again thought, *FIRE!*

A bolt of fire streamed from her fingertips and the Russian's head exploded. Pieces of his skull and brains clung to the hallway walls and floor.

Jon Sommers stood above the Russian, looking his own 9mm Beretta. No smoke wafted from its barrel. He looked at the headless dead body, and then at Ann.

Jon shook his head with disbelief. "Hello, Ann. Neat trick. Are you unharmed?"

She was still in shock and couldn't speak. She took inventory. No wounds anywhere on her body. She nodded and smiled.

When she could once again speak, she said, "What now?"

"Your trick. It's our little secret. For me, it's back into the stairwell. I'm scouring the floors for hostiles at work. For you, stay hidden. I promise I'll return soon." Jon headed back the way he'd come.

Ann continued to monitor the action from her view of the security cams. She heard the shots diminish in frequency until there were none. Cassie's voice said, "We're done. Let's make sure Strumler is alive."

Ann took the elevator to the lobby. As she emerged, she saw a group of men wearing FBI jackets enter the same elevator she'd exited.

Ann sat in one of the plush armchairs in the lobby and waited for the inevitable. Her body began to shake more and more violently. She reached into her backpack and pulled a bag of sour gummies from it. After eating the entire bag's contents, the shaking began to subside.

She was beginning to feel normal when the elevator doors opened again. The FBI agents emerged from the elevator leading Strumler in handcuffs. The president-elect was screaming, "I'll sue you for this! I'll sue you all!"

It was all over. She shook herself to loosen her cramping legs and arms.

* * *

A few days had passed since the president-elect's arrest.

Ann was back at the Stanford campus, looking at the grades posted in the Student Union lobby. She grinned when she discovered she had aced her midterm on computer forensics. After attending her afternoon classes, she walked back to her apartment and passed a newsstand.

The headline on one of the newspapers stated, "Strumler to Be Tried for Treason." She decided to read the news online when she had reached her apartment.

When she unlocked the door, she heard someone humming in her kitchen. The familiar voice belonged to Laura Hunter. "Hi, Ann. Did you get my message?"

"Ah, no, Laura. I just returned from a trip back east. What's in your message?"

"Me. Paraguay didn't work out. I'm back, attending Stanford. I assume you'll still let me be your roommate?"

Ann smiled. "Sure."

She turned on the television and watched the continuing story of the pending trial of Daniel Strumler. She thought, *it's even better on-screen than it was when I was there.*

Laura cooked them dinner. While Laura was busy, Ann called Cassie.

Her mother answered the call, but after Ann said hello, Cassie's voice turned loud and angry. "You told me you'd stay safe. But you didn't do what you promised. You behaved like a child."

"Mom. I'm sorry. I know it was irresponsible of me. I promise I'll never disappoint you like that again."

"Bullshit, Ann. How can I trust you?"

"Yeah. Well, I thought I was in a safe place. I was wrong."

"Crap. Well, okay. Did you get your midterm grades?"

"Yeah. I did fine. And Laura's back. So it's pretty much back to normal."

"I like normal." She heard Cassie laugh.

Ann smiled. Her mom had already let her anger go.

* * *

Avram Shimmel was once again back at work at the United Nations. His brief assignment as an acting ambassador to the United Nations was over. He couldn't say he missed being a diplomat, since his entire career until this assignment had been in the military.

He made himself comfortable in his overstuffed office chair as he admired the view from his office window. The East River sat twenty-nine floors beneath him, the streets due west of him filled with skyscrapers. It was an unseasonably warm day and he saw pedestrians wearing light jackets as they walked the sidewalks below.

His phone buzzed. "Shimmel here."

"It's Meyer. Our UN ambassador has resigned. She was unhappy that you delivered a speech she had wanted to make, and she decided to run for a seat in the Knesset. We are currently without a United Nations ambassador. The PM suggested you."

"Me? I'm not a diplomat!"

"Yes. Are you deaf?"

"But who will run the UN Paramilitary Force?"

"That's a problem for you to solve. What's your answer?"

Avram knew that there was no way he could deny a command assigned to him by the Israeli PM. He sighed. "I accept."

"Good. You will be stationed at the Israeli embassy in New

York. Report there as soon as you can." Meyer terminated the call.

Jon Sommers' office was adjacent to Avram's, albeit somewhat smaller. Avram called Jon's line. "Sommers."

"Jon, drop by my office as soon as you have a moment."

Jon recognized Avram's thick Israeli accent. "On my way now."

He walked in, smiling, and took a seat. "What's up?"

"I've been asked by Israel's PM to accept the position of Israeli ambassador to the United Nations."

"Wow. Congrats, big guy. That's quite a coup."

"Maybe, maybe, but it leaves me with a problem. I have to replace myself. Do you have any preference as to who becomes your next boss?"

Jon's face showed surprise and confusion. "I've not had time to digest this."

"Well, if there is no one you'd prefer for your next boss, then I guess I'll just have to appoint you. Congratulations, you are now director of the UN Paramilitary Force."

Avram saw Jon's eyes bulge. It was all Avram could do to keep a grin off his face. But within a second, he could no longer help himself. His own smile beamed back at his friend. Jon had been a Mossad *kidon*, or assassin, and had plenty of experience working within the halls of a bureaucratic empire.

Jon shrugged. "You sure about this? I've never commanded anything larger than an operations team. Five at most."

Avram nodded. "Congrats. You're it. I have to leave now and start preparations to move my office to the embassy. Good luck, my friend."

Avram rose, shook Jon's hand and walked from his—now former—office.

Jon turned and faced Avram's receding form. "Wait. What's my job description?"

Avram stopped, turned, and faced Jon. "You'll figure it out, just as I did."

An hour passed, with Jon unable to move from his seat across from Avram's desk. No. Now it was Jon's desk.

He rose and reseated himself in his new chair. He was too short for its current setting. Jon adjusted the seat until he was finally comfortable. He opened the desk drawers and pulled all the folders from it. It took him through the day and long into the evening to read them, open the computer's file directory and take inventory of the contents.

He sent a text message to Ann.

As the sun set and the night stars shone over Manhattan, Jon Sommers smiled and thought to himself, *I wonder if this promotion will turn out to be a blessing or a curse?*

* * *

Ann's cell buzzed as she entered her computer audit procedures class. She read the text and smiled:

> Ann—Thanks for saving my life. Don't worry about your secret. I expect we'll work together again, soon and often.—Jon

Ann thought, *yes, Jon. Now you owe me one and I owe you one.*

TEN MONTHS LATER

CHAPTER 2

Cecil H. Green Library,
557 Escondido Mall, Stanford University, CA

September 3, 10:14 a.m.

Ann Sashakovich walked from the parking lot adjacent to the Hoover Tower toward what she thought of as "the main library" and thought, *it's good to be back*. She smiled like a child who had just recovered a long-lost beloved toy. Stanford University didn't smile back. The library stood, cloisters gleaming stucco beige, topped with an orange-tiled roof in the warm September afternoon. She'd arrived one day early for the school semester, to give herself time to adjust past the jetlag of her flight from Washington, DC, where Cassie and Lee, her adopted parents lived. She walked around the campus, savoring memories of her previous years as an undergrad.

The quad was mostly empty of students, many not having yet arrived. She basked in the still, dry heat that was common in Northern California this time of year. She hoped this year would be less eventful than her sophomore year when she'd barely escaped with her life from a series of unexpected adventures.

The stress from the unpleasant adventure during her sophomore year had led her to eat far too much unhealthy food. As a result, she knew she'd packed on a few extra pounds. She'd vowed to lose the weight, but that hadn't happened. She still had occasional nightmares from being in the wrong place at the wrong time last year. She hadn't intended on battling Russian commandos in the Strumler Tower in Washington, DC, as they took floor after floor.

Her frequent nightmares were an accurate rendition of the real event, and her life had been saved by a special ability she had developed after she'd been overdosed with Bug-Lok nanodevices. Her ability to shoot bolts of energy from her fingertips only worked when she was angry. And each time she used that special ability, it left her exhausted and hungry, shaking violently to the point of being unable even to stand up. She'd vowed to avoid situations where she might be tempted again to summon her special talent. And, so far, she had succeeded.

She entered one of the many cafeterias, passed the electronic bulletin-board display and read the notices flowing by on the rolling screen. One of the notices held her interest so much that she stayed there and reread it several times:

Build a Sentient AI Computer for DARPA.
Grand Prize: $1,000,000
The Defense Advanced Research Projects Agency
announces its autumn hackathon competition:
a $1,000,000 first prize to the group that can
demonstrate a sentient artificial intelligence
entity. Two other prizes of $250,000 each will be

awarded to groups that show major advances in
the functioning of artificial intelligence. Our most
important objective is an entity that can keep
national defense computers from being hacked. The
system must be able to recode itself without human
help as new threats emerge.

There was more content, including rules and due dates, plus instructions on how to apply. Ann thought, *just like DARPA to post an automation tech contest on a public bulletin board.* She knew that Stanford also offered students seed funding to produce advances in AI using "undergraduate research opportunities," but DARPA's was a more intensive approach.

She turned away and walked to the campus bookstore to buy the textbooks for this semester's classes. She thought of the irony: her first class tomorrow was CS 221, Artificial Intelligence: Principles and Techniques.

She wondered if she was up to the DARPA challenge. It would obviously require a team. But how could she find other students who might work with her? Last year, she had watched her now-ex-boyfriend, Glen Sarkov, as his team sought funding for their startup, MindField, Inc. It had ended in a disaster that almost cost Glen his life. Ann took a deep breath and thought about what running a team might entail. If she tried and failed, the experience would teach her valuable lessons. As the day progressed, she found herself returning to thoughts of entering the contest.

The next day, Ann attended her first classes of the semester. Her second class, at 10:00 in the morning, was CS 229, Machine Learning. As a junior-year information-science major at Stanford, Ann had several of her classes as seminars in smaller rooms, and only two classes, including this one, in auditoriums.

Since she was five-foot-six, even if she sat in the first row she knew she wouldn't block anyone else's view. She selected a seat a bit left of the classroom's center, but close to the lectern so she could better see the professor.

The class started and Professor Myron Uretsky droned on about the history of computing and how it inevitably led to the current situation in which people used artificially intelligent tools in their homes and in their everyday lives.

Ann's thoughts drifted once again to the DARPA contest. What would her "team" look like? What skills would be required? How would her team differ from Glen's startup company?

When the professor stopped and announced their homework, Ann's attention snapped back into the room and she stared at the whiteboard. *An assignment after the first class?* She pulled up the syllabus on her notebook computer. *No assignment mentioned there.* She assessed the amount of time she'd need to complete it and cursed silently. *There go both evenings between now and my next machine-learning class.* She rose from the desk and packed her notebook computer into her backpack. *Off to my last class of the day, Neurochemical Biology.*

She crossed under the cloistered overhangs into the quadrangle and headed across the lawn toward the path that would take her to the set of temporary classroom buildings among the oak trees, south of where her first class was. As she entered into one of the wooden structures and headed up the staircase, she bumped into someone and nearly dropped her backpack. One of her textbooks fell to the ground.

She looked up at the tall man who'd bumped into her. Standing at least six inches taller than her was her ex-boyfriend from last year, Glen Sarkov. He frowned, his gaze refocusing on Ann as if he had just become conscious. "Ann? Sorry. Didn't mean to... I, um, oops. You okay?" He picked up her fallen textbook and handed it back to her.

She frowned. "Yeah. Okay." She tried to move past him but he intentionally blocked her path.

"A second, please."

She frowned again. "Sure. How are you, Glen?"

"I haven't seen you since last June. What're you up to?"

"Just classes. And homework." She thought about asking after his own situation, but decided not to encourage him. After all, they were no longer "a thing." She pouted, thinking how much he'd disappointed her. "Got to get to my class."

"Sure. Look, maybe we can get together for a drink some-time?"

She stared back at him, remembering how he'd used her to attract Samantha, a cofounder of his startup. And then, he'd ended his relationship with Ann. She decided not to consider his offer. *Like that could ever happen.* "Maybe."

She walked along the hallway of the second floor to her last class. By the time she arrived, most of the seats were taken. She sat on the floor at the back of the room. She'd thought she would find neurochemical biology interesting. But, when the syllabus was distributed by the professor, she scanned its pages and realized the class would just be very difficult.

She overheard some of the students in the room talking to each other. She instantly realized that most of the other students in this class had previously taken courses in biochemistry or advanced psychology. Her background was in information science. She'd hoped this class would give her knowledge she could use in how humans and computer systems were similar, but the syllabus made it clear to her that all she'd be learning were long chemical formulas and how chemicals affected neural clusters. She was immediately both bored and intimidated.

She opened her bookbag and pulled out her notebook computer. She turned on the recording app to complement her notes, not really expecting to understand much. She thought, *I'd have had better luck with a course in Mandarin.*

After class, she plodded over a mile from campus down University Avenue to her apartment, which wasn't air conditioned. But she found the cool staircase up to her flat was a welcome relief. She could smell cleaning fluid as she opened the door to her apartment. Her roommate, Laura Hunter, was on her knees, scouring the floor.

Ann sniffed the air and wrinkled her nose. "Why are you doing that?"

Laura looked up briefly, then back at the floor. "Spots. Spots on the floor." She continued scrubbing.

Ann couldn't see any stains on the linoleum. She shook her head. Since Laura's return from Paraguay last year, the young woman had developed a compulsive streak. Ann opened the fridge and pulled out a container of yogurt. She grabbed a spoon and sat on the couch. "I saw something interesting on the old bulletin board outside the student union. A contest."

Laura stopped cleaning. Her blonde head popped up. "What contest?"

"It's being sponsored by the Feds. They want a team to create a sentient artificial intelligence."

"Oh. You mean like in the movie *Terminator*?"

"Zackly."

"Life imitates art.

"Maybe. Anyway, I'm thinking of recruiting a team to enter the contest."

"You need a team? Like the one your boyfriend Glen had last year? Don't you think that's too dangerous? After the government funded Glen's startup last year, they tried to kill him. Sure you want to do this?"

Ann's hand left the spoon inside the yogurt container and wandered to her chin. She stroked it as she thought about the risk. DARPA was mostly toothless and their hackathons were always well received. She'd never heard of any of the entrants meeting a bad end. "I dunno. Probably not."

She spent the rest of the evening writing the homework assignment for her artificial intelligence class. Her premise was how long and how much development would be required before AIs could become sentient. She read several online articles, among them "AI 100: The Artificial Intelligence Startups Redefining Industries," published by cbinsights.com. There was enough information within this article to give her a list of all the skills that might be required to form an effective and competitive team for the DARPA contest. When she finished the first draft of her paper, it was after ten. She had an early class the next morning, so Ann plodded off to bed.

When she woke the next morning, all she could think of was the damned DARPA contest. She bolted out of bed and was in the bathroom before Laura woke.

Then she dressed, heated leftover coffee in the microwave, and trotted along University Avenue through Palo Alto and back to the campus. While she hurried across the overpass bridge, she thought about who she could get to sponsor the additional funding a team might need if they were headed into the DARPA contest. After all, Stanford might not give her enough cash and there might be other things she'd need to acquire if she were to compete.

But she couldn't even decide whether or not to enter. When she reached the quad, she decided to speak with her adoptive parents. *Cassie and Lee might offer an informed answer*.

Ann headed from the cafeteria to the hallway outside the Cecil H. Green Library.

It was quiet there, very few people walking in and out. She pulled her cellphone from her pocket and punched in her folks' number. Cassie answered on the first ring.

"Hi, mom. I need advice."

"Wow, that's a first. Are you sure you're okay?"

"Yeah. Anyway, DARPA has posted a hackathon contest and I'm thinking of entering."

"What's the contest for? And why? Won't this take time away from your studies?"

"Maybe. But I have at least one class in the topic that forms the backbone of the contest. They want groups to compete in developing a sentient AI."

"Oh, crap. My daughter is gonna try to build Data, the *Star Trek* robot."

"Well, yeah."

"Ann, let me remind you that these DARPA nightmares are a waste of time. Last year it was the GNU radio. The year before, it was drone warfare. Their contests are about producing better technology for warfare. Are you sure you want to be a part of that?"

"Well, that's just it, mom. I don't know. The prize is a shitload of cash. Plus the notoriety. So, I'm guessing you'd advise me to pass. Right?"

She could hear Cassie breathing but no words for a long time. "I know you'll do the opposite of what I tell you. You always do."

Ann struggled to keep from chuckling. "Probably."

"Would you like to hear your father's opinion before you decide?"

Ann smiled. Cassie had once been a spy, but Lee worked in computer security. "Yes!"

"Wait. I'll get him. He's in the garage with your grandfather. They're fixing the roadster."

Ann heard her footsteps. Then she heard a voice. Not her father.

Her grandfather. "Hello, sweet child. What you learning at school, *pozhaluysta*."

"Hi, Kiril. Just studying. When did you get into town?"

"Two days ago. You know, I live less than an hour from your school. You could drive to the coast and visit. Maybe soon, *da*?"

"Okay. I promise. Is Lee there?"

Lee took the phone. "Hi, sweetie. So Cassie told me you're thinking about entering a DARPA contest. My advice is that, if you do, be careful picking your team. Startups are subject to a host of backfires and miscues. And, in a burgeoning field like AI, the obstacles for a brand-new team could become insurmountable."

"But, you're not advising me to stay out of the contest? Right?"

"No. It's your decision. But just know that what you're considering is difficult. You'll have competition that is every bit as bright as you are."

Ann thought in silence. "Okay. Thanks, dad." She terminated the call and headed toward the cafeteria for lunch.

As she walked, realized that whether or not she entered the contest, she'd been very lucky so far in her life. From the day her birthmother overdosed on crack, leaving her and her younger brother orphaned, she'd countered every setback with something she learned that still held value. She was twelve then, and had needed someplace to hide from the social services department of New York City. She and Joshua took refuge among the homeless in the endless warren of tunnels underneath Grand Central Station. But lost within the vast labyrinth of cramped tunnels, Joshua was murdered by a homeless man, who then raped her. Even this setback led to meeting Cassandra Sashakovich later that night. Months later, Cassie returned to the tunnels and adopted Ann, saving her from life among the homeless. So far, things seemed always to turn out okay for her.

She took a breath to clear her mind before she walked through the nearest cafeteria's doors.

She filled a tray with food and coffee, then found an empty table and sat. The ham sandwich was dry and tasteless but she gobbled it down anyway. The coffee was burned and too hot so she sipped and shuddered. She saw a shadow looming over her from behind.

Glen Sarkov. He sat across from her. "Look, I get it. You're still angry with me."

She decided to drive the point home. Like a dagger, she stared at him and said, "How is Samantha Trout?" Glen had dumped Ann for Samantha, his chief financial officer.

Glen shrugged. "We ran out of money before we completed the prototype. And, it turns out that the president-elect owned the VC firm that invested in us. So, after he was arrested for treason, our startup became evidence in his trial. We were screwed! Sam was angry with all of us. She just left me and told me to fuck off. Turns out, Sam was only after me for my stock shares."

"So, MindField was a total failure?"

Glen shrugged "Most entrepreneurs go through several failed startups before they are successful with one. So maybe I'm on my way now."

Ann nodded. She still doubted she could suffer Glen as her friend.

CHAPTER 3

Ann Sashakovich's apartment,
#211, 3950 Louis Road, Palo Alto, CA

September 4, 7:36 a.m.

The next day, Ann slept through her wakeup alarm. She bumbled her way into the bathroom and saw that the way she'd slept on her hair left her with a long brown spike rising from the middle of her head. She tried brushing it, but to no avail. Hair spray softened the spike, but her hair still looked weird. She dropped her head under the tap of the bathroom sink and then dried it. Much better.

She rushed along University Avenue with the sun beating down and perspiration dripping along her neck and arms. According to her wristwatch, she would arrive at least ten minutes late to her early morning class: SYMSYS 261, Applied Symbolic Systems: Venture Capital, Artificial Intelligence, and the Future.

She sneaked into the back of the classroom, feeling breathless. She sat in the back row and took notes diligently as the professor spoke at the lectern. Her mind drifted occasionally but was quickly drawn back each time by the professor's references to team formation, reminding her of the DARPA contest.

Several of the students asked questions that led Ann to believe they were also pondering whether to enter the contest. *Maybe it's just my overactive imagination.*

After the class, she exited the auditorium, following two of the other students who'd asked these provocative questions. She heard them mention DARPA and now wondered if most of her competition would be from this very class.

Ann found a place to sit in one of the Green Library's carrels and started a list of the positions she would need to fill to complete her team, were she to enter. Due to her experience with Glen's startup last year, she thought of the team as if it were a startup. She'd need a CEO, CFO, CTO, VP Personnel, and VP Marketing, but she was sure most of the gut-work staffing would be the programmers reporting to the CTO. Probably at least fifteen total headcount for her team in the contest. Maybe even more.

Ann tried to think of people other than classmates she knew who could fill these roles. She wondered if she could interest her mentor, William Wing, in the CTO job? Wing was a legendary hacker, his name spoken in whispers among the cyberpunk community.

Wasn't William working with Betsy Brown for Jon Sommers at the UN's paramilitary force in New York?

She called William and he picked up on the third ring,

"Cybersecurity, Director Wing Speaking."

"William, it's Ann Sashakovich."

"Ann? How are things out on the wrong coast?"

"Fine, but I'd like to ask a favor."

"Kinda busy. But ask away, maybe I can help. If not, maybe I know someone who can."

"I'm thinking of entering a DARPA contest. They want a sentient AI. I'd like to offer you the CTO job."

He laughed. "Been there. Done that. Why would I want to try to do it again?"

"Do you know someone who could help out? It's only for a few months."

"So sorry, no. And it will probably turn out to take two or three times as much time as I have to find you the proper candidate to do this. My advice is to walk away, and fast. Listen, I've got to go. One of our pen tests just triggered a virus. But, thanks for asking."

She sat in the nearest chair and dropped her head into her hands. *Nothing is easy. Maybe William is right. Maybe I should just complete my studies.*

But now, she couldn't stop thinking about the DARPA contest. William's opinion had her redoubling her concentration on the contest.

She knew she'd need an entire team of people at least as smart as her mentor.

Who? And how could she find cofounders? What if she underestimated the amount of funding she requested from Stanford?

She opened her notebook to the Stanford University Catalog and in the index she found an entry on Student Research Projects: CS 294A, titled "Research Project in Artificial Intelligence." It would earn her 3 units. She reread the course description.

> Student teams under faculty supervision work on
> research and implementation of a large project in
> AI. State-of-the-art methods related to the problem

domain. Prerequisites: AI course from 220 series,
and consent of instructor.

She already knew that the university offered funding and
facilities for student research projects described as "independent study." She read the notes below the description and
found that the university could help her recruit team members
from the MBA program to fill non-tech positions. *I'm gonna
do this!*

She called the university registrar and set an appointment
to meet and discuss how this might work for her and her team.
Now she'd be playing the waiting game.

CHAPTER 4

**Wilbur Dining Hall, Stanford University,
658 Escondido Road, Palo Alto, CA**

September 4, 1:32 p.m.

As Ann ate a quick lunch at the Star Ginger dining room of Wilbur Dining facility, she heard her cellphone buzzing in her bookbag. She pulled the cell out too late; the call had vanished into voicemail. She saw that Glen had called. She frowned, but still found herself hitting the button to call him back.

"It's Ann. What do you want?"

"I'm sorry, but it's my nature to be persistent. Can we spend a few minutes pretending we're still friends?"

"I'm not sure that's even possible. But, okay. I'll give it a try."

"Where are you right now?"

"The Wilbur."

"I'll be there in less than a minute." She waited at her table until she saw him walk up the steps. She waved so he could see her at her table in the middle of the cafeteria. A large group of students sat at the next table and began talking and shouting. This had suddenly turned into a noisy place to meet.

Glen's voice showed his nervousness. He spoke for just a

few seconds and she couldn't hear his words over the din. She heard the last word: "Dinner?"

"I'm busy with papers and studying."

"But it's just dinner. Think of it as a free meal and conversation with someone you were close to last year." Glen smiled at Ann. "You already know me. I'm not a bad person, even if I mistreated you once. I promise I won't ever do that again. Ever. How about it?"

Ann thought about Glen. He'd been good to her through most of their relationship. She'd grown to trust him and even moved into his apartment. But, then he'd dumped her for Samantha. Could she forgive him? "Why do you think it will be any different for us this time?"

"Oh, yeah, I understand your concern. Sam was nothing but trouble. I think what I want now is a real relationship. Give and take. Someone I can trust."

She wondered if he really meant he wanted someone he could control. But, if she was careful and took it one small step at a time, maybe it could work. "Okay, Glen. I'll give you another chance. But know that I doubt you can prove to me that you're trustworthy."

"Dinner tonight. Nothing heavy. How about pizza at the Stanford Shopping Mall?"

After the sun set, Ann and Glen met at the California Pizza Kitchen, a casual restaurant with pizza, pasta, and soda on the menu. Glen bought a small margherita pizza and they sat on metal chairs at a Formica table.

He looked directly into her eyes. "What professors do you have this semester?" Ann noted that he started the conversation referencing what she'd already told him was most important to her.

"Haven't thought much about my classes yet. My room-mate from last year, Laura, is still a bit batty, but I think she's recovered from her misadventure in Paraguay. Some of my classwork so far is tedious but the AI class is pretty provocative. How are you doing in the wake of your MindField debacle?"

"It wasn't a debacle. I learned tons about how to manage a growing company. Now, I'm ready for the CEO position I had then. Failure taught me a lot."

Ann nodded. "Really? So you believe failure is a great teacher."

He nodded, his face set as if this was some monumental insight.

She wondered if it was a lesson or if he really thought it was just "bad joss," a Chinese term for luck she'd picked up from William Wing. Then something more important rose up in her mind. Would she always be just someone to pass the time with if they renewed their friendship? Or, even worse, their relationship. "Glen, what do you plan to do in June after you've graduated?" She would need to understand any hidden implications of his answer to this question.

"Either work at a venture capital firm or find venture capi-tal to fund a startup of my own."

"So, essentially, try again at what you just failed at, until you get it right. Yes?"

Glen seemed to ponder this. "Umm, pretty much. Ann, being your own boss is something that's impossible to forget. For one thing, all the mistakes I made are ones I'll avoid. And don't forget that other most companies are unlikely to hire someone as staff once they've had the top position. I pretty much blew away any other jobs."

Ann nodded. She'd never thought about Glen's prospects

this way before. "What if I told you that being with you while you ran MindField was terribly unpleasant for me."

"That's no big surprise. But remember that I'm smarter now. I promise I'll treat you better. I promise I'll take your opinion into consideration with every choice I make."

She had doubts he could. She was sure he wouldn't. She doubted he was capable of considering the needs of anyone close to him. She wasn't sure things could ever be this simple. She wondered if Samantha had found him to be a caring lover.

She had to decide if she wanted to be with him despite her doubts. More important to her was his inability in the past to be faithful to her. She remembered how duplicitous he was when she moved into his apartment last year. She decided to test him. "What about the fact that you cheated on me?"

He looked as he might have if she'd slapped his face. When he answered, his eyes looked away and toward the floor. An indicator that he wasn't being honest. "I'm sorry. I promise it will never happen again."

She felt as if the room had suddenly gotten much smaller. She stopped speaking and tried to think. Could he really take her needs seriously? But, she still found him attractive; an itch she wanted to scratch. "Last year, when we had sex, it was totally dissatisfying. You paid no attention to me and what I wanted. Did you and Sam have sex?"

He looked down and to the left again, probably lying. "Yeah. Several times."

"Did you get her to climax?"

Glen's jaw dropped. "Well, I guess so."

"That's a 'no,' then, Glen."

"What makes you so sure?"

"Tell me, exactly what did you do to her, to push her toward orgasm. And what you asked in return?"

"Listen, Ann, this conversation is making me uncomfortable. What gives you the right to ask me about my sex life with another woman?"

"You have one chance to convince me you'll be considerate. Consider this a job interview."

Glen's expression showed shock, softening with understanding. "Really?"

"Yup. Last time we had sex, it felt as if you were in a different world from me. I've had better sex masturbating."

He pushed back from the table. "I think we're done, Ann."

She shook her head. "Whatever."

She watched him leave the restaurant, wondering what to do about him.

CHAPTER 5

Ann Sashakovich's apartment,
#211, 3950 Louis Road, Palo Alto, CA

September 4, 10:36 p.m.

Lying in bed, Ann was once again finding sleep evading her. Even after masturbating, she was unable to force her mind from boil to simmer. All she could think about was her conversation with Glen. She forced herself to think about anything else. What flew into her mind was the DARPA contest.

The deadline for applications was looming and she realized that if she was going to enter, she'd have to file within the next three days. She still didn't even have any of the positions filled, let alone a fully configured team.

She knew she had one major advantage over anyone else who competed in the contest: Ann had been closer to AI circuitry than anyone else alive. She'd been modified through having had nearly a thousand Bug-Lok nanodevices fed into her brain by the CypherGhost nearly two years ago. Even though the nanodevices had expired and left her body, their leftover result had been that she'd developed the ability to use parts of her brain no one else could use. And she could shoot bolts of energy from her fingertips. She embodied the very essence of being a cyborg. Not that far from AI.

But all that means nothing if I can't alter my abilities into understanding thinking circuits outside myself. She tried deep breathing to place her in a meditative trance, hoping it would turn into a sleep state, but that didn't work. As she finally started to drift off, her alarm buzzed. The night had ended without her falling asleep.

She rushed through washing up and swallowing coffee, then trotted to her AI class, where she sat next to a red-haired young man who smiled awkwardly at her.

He extended his hand. "I'm Dave Nordman."

She noted his rumpled clothing. "Ann Sashakovich. How are you doing with the class homework assignment?"

"Well, this class is my fave. The homework is fun." He brushed back a lock of scarlet hair that fell instantly back in front of his eyes. "How about you?"

She smiled. "Yeah. So far, it's the only one this semester that might be fun."

"Before Stanford, I was a motherboard designer. I'm wondering how much a circuit board is really capable of. Have you seen the DARPA contest?"

Ann's eyes snapped toward Nordman's face. "It's probably the most all-consuming thing on the tech part of campus. So, yeah. You thinking of entering?"

He frowned. "I'd love to, but I don't think I have the leadership skills. I'm just a hacker."

"Listen, I'm interested in leading a team. May I have your cellphone?"

He reached tentatively into his pocket while she opened hers to her "contacts" screen.

She sent her contact info to him. "Call me after class when you have time. Maybe we can do business."

Early that evening, he called her. "So I guess you're entering the contest. Well, if you're thinking of me as one of your team members, I, ah, see myself as a creator, not a leader. I can manage people well enough, but I'm not going to ever be a CEO. I don't want the headaches. Could you see me as your CTO?"

Ann thought about him. Clumsy, drab, but possibly good in this role.

"Dave, let me think about it. But I am interested."

"Good, then. I'll wait for your decision."

After the phone call, she took out her notebook computer and started a file called "DARPA Contest Org Chart."

She already knew who she wanted as her chief marketing officer. She called Samantha Trout. Sam may have been Glen's girlfriend, but Ann had seen her in action. While Samantha was pursuing a major in finance, Ann knew Samantha was a natural at marketing and she seemed to have no desire to lead a team.

"Hi, it's Ann Sashakovich. How are you and can we meet?"

"Why?"

"I'm starting a team for the DARPA contest. I'm looking for a CMO."

She heard Sam laugh. "So starting companies really is contagious. You caught it from that bastard Sarkov."

"We can talk over lunch if you're interested. How about dim sum?"

She heard Sam sigh. "Whatever. Remember that I'm a finance major, not a marketing major. But, a free meal works for me. Tomorrow."

They met at Tai Pan, an elegant restaurant on Waverley Street, off University Avenue.

Ann had forgotten that Samantha was gorgeous. Ann found it impossible to stop staring at the Eurasian woman's enormous eyes and tiny nose. Sam's lips were pink pillows of soft flesh. Ann found speech difficult at first.

They sat and Samantha said, "When you called last night, at first I thought you just wanted to pick my brain about Glen."

"Glen? No. Not interested in a relationship with Glen. For one thing, he isn't ready. You're proof of that. For another, if I want a relationship, it'll be with someone who has more answers and raises fewer questions. No one in my life currently fits that bill."

"Then why are we here? Surely you didn't just want to know if I knew someone who could fill your CMO position. Or is it just about the dim sum?"

"It's exactly as I told you. No games. I'm thinking of starting an AI company. I'd like your help."

Sam's head shifted forward and sideways just a little. "Me? I was just involved in a big-assed failure." She smiled and stared into Ann's eyes. "I thought you might be gay."

Ann felt her eyes bulge just a little. "No. I mean, not sure about that one. I've fucked both sexes. But no, not interested."

"Too bad. From what Glen told me, you're a handful."

"Would you be at all interested in being part of a DARPA contest team?"

"And do what? You need another trained monkey? But, tell you what. You give me some details. I might sign an NDA. Then, if I'm still not interested, I'll give you my best advice for a board seat and some stock. Deal?"

Ann didn't have to think about the deal. "Done." But she

didn't yet have an NDA document. "I'll send you the doc tomorrow by email."

Ann hoped that Sam would decide to join her team, but now she doubted it would ever happen. As she left the restaurant, she wondered if she was the first DARPA contest team leader who'd approached Sam.

CHAPTER 6

Cecil H. Green Library,
557 Escondido Mall, Stanford University, CA

September 5, 1:57 p.m.

Ann called Sam after she finished lunch.

"Ann," said Sam, "I've read the DARPA contest rules and thought about your offer. Your only market is the military, and that would be boring for me. The way it stands now, well, there isn't anything attractive enough there for me."

"What would you like?"

"I'm willing to stand in for you until you find a suitable CMO for up to three weeks, for an offer of three percent founder's shares."

Ann thought about what this would look like to a venture capitalist. "That would make it a lot more difficult if we decide to use the contest as the precursor for an IPO. I can't give someone what amounts to one percent stock per week."

"What can you offer? It better be your best offer."

Ann thought about how much stock she could bleed to get the chance to understand Samantha's views on the market for AI devices. "How about half what you want? One-and-a-half percent?"

"Let me think about it. I'll let you know tomorrow."

Ann was running short of time to place a complete management team into her DARPA contest application. "You have until eight in the morning. After that, I'll have to pencil in someone else's name."

"Okay, Ann. Bye."

Ann wondered if Sam would decide to join as her CMO. She had no backup plan to find a CTO and worried that, without a candidate, her application would show a blank for this crucial role. Moreover, she wondered if Sam had the energy to push customer concerns into the project. From her adopted mother and father, Ann knew the military, their primary customer, was both fickle and demanding.

But the crush of time led her to decide to continue her search for a permanent CMO.

* * *

Ann sat at a carrel in Green Library. The university registrar's office still hadn't returned her call. She might have to revise her assumptions about the level of support Stanford could offer her.

She opened her notebook, pulled up the DARPA website, and started to fill in the DARPA contest application. But, she stopped dead when she came to the blanks for her team member names. She reviewed her list of potential cofounders.

Ann would be team leader, the equivalent of a corporate CEO. She wasn't sure she was the best of her group for this role, but that didn't matter yet. If someone better showed up, she was prepared to sponsor them as team leader. If that happened, she would occupy a more technical role.

Sam had volunteered to act as the team's stand-in for CMO, but Ann hadn't given up on trying to convince Sam to accept the position permanently. Sam hadn't been responsible for the failure of MindField, since the startup never got to the point where they actually had something to sell. Ann could always change this field in the application if Sam left after three weeks.

Dave Nordman would be the CTO. He'd never been part of any startup, but he had been the technical lead on hardware for several Silicon Valley chip and board producers.

Ann still needed a human resources head. This was the one area where she knew of no one with the appropriate skills.

But there was no time left to her if she wanted to be part of the DARPA contest.

She left the fields for "Human Resources Lead" and "Finance Lead" blank. She had just contacted several candidates to select from for each of these two positions. And several had returned her phone calls.

She looked at the following positions in the DARPA application:

> Team Lead: Ann Sashakovich
> Technical Lead: David Nordman
> Finance Lead:
> Marketing Lead: Samantha Trout
> Human Resources Lead:

She filled in the remainder of the DARPA application. She decided to hit the Enter key now, and then head over to the registrar's office to see it they could assist in staffing her team. After acknowledging receipt of her application, the page shifted to a subpage containing a list of the competitors in the contest.

She scrolled down the list of teams registered and saw Glen Sarkov's name. *Damn! We're competitors. I misjudged him again. What do I do now?* She thought of calling him, but what could she say? She knew what she wanted to tell him, but that would change nothing,

She thought, as she closed her notebook and started walking toward the administration building, that she felt just a bit as Julius Caesar had as he crossed the Rubicon.

* * *

The registrar's office was friendly enough but not very helpful. An elderly woman told her to go to the student research-project director's office, two floors up.

She waited nearly an hour to see someone.

A tall, slender man with a scruffy beard smiled and extended his hand. "I'm Edgar Turnbull. How can I assist you?"

Ann smiled back and they shook hands. "I'm interested in staffing a research team."

"Ah. Well, sorry for the wait. That damned DARPA contest has everyone looking for team members."

Ann was silent for a few seconds. "Me too. I'll need a finance lead and a human resources lead. I might also need a marketing lead."

Turnbull frowned. "We're backed up looking for those skills. It might take a few days. Can you wait that long?"

Ann nodded. "Yes, if I have to."

"You'll need to fill in some forms." He pulled two forms off his desktop. "Sign this one and give it to me now, then use this one to visit the link on the paper and fill in the one describing your available positions. After that, it will be up to the business school's student body."

She left his office feeling hopeful for the first time.

* * *

The Russian president sat patiently while one of his staff applied makeup to his face. He stayed as motionless as possible until the woman nodded.

He rose and walked to the cameraman standing near the stage. "You know what I want. Let's get this in one take. I have a busy schedule today."

The cameraman nodded and the prime oligarch stepped behind the lectern, his eyes fixed on the teleprompter as the screen flashed numbers, counting down the seconds until the broadcast.

"Good evening, fellow citizens. Tonight I am most pleased to announce that Russia is currently amassing an army that is undefeatable in battle. Our country has over thirty thousand armored mobile robots, equipped with artificial intelligence, ready for battle with any enemy foolish enough to engage us.

"No longer will Russian citizens risk their lives fighting, as we have had to do for centuries when invaders threatened us.

"These robots are armored with titanium and outfitted with hack-proof silicon circuitry. They are impervious to weather and virtually indestructible. We are manufacturing them at plants throughout the country at a rate of nearly a thousand every day. By the end of this year we will have a complete army of them, and by the end of next year the army will be five-hundred thousand strong.

"Be proud, my fellow citizens." He pointed to the space near him, and the camera moved to show a seven-foot-tall metallic monster with red LED eyes. The robot saluted the Russian president and then stood at attention, staring at the camera.

The president smiled and stared into the camera as the video ended.

* * *

Ann watched the television news that evening and saw the reporter translate what the Russian president had announced several hours before. *Is the DARPA contest set up to enable the United States to fight a cyberwar using artificial-intelligence-driven robots instead of human soldiers? What will happen when robot armies fight each other? What will happen to governments when they don't see a human cost in war?*

She had read statements from Musk, Gates, and Hawking claiming artificial intelligence could end humanity. The doubts that had then been planted in her mind sprouted once again as she thought about the havoc a weaponized AI army could wreak. The very project that her team would be designing. *If we succeed, could humanity ever recover?*

CHAPTER 7

Ann Sashakovich's apartment,
#211, 3950 Louis Road, Palo Alto, CA

September 5, 10:01 p.m.

Ann sat in silence, measuring the probabilities and possibilities of what might occur if her team succeeded, versus any other team. *It's best if we win and incorporate some AI version of ethics and morality into our code.* She envisioned their product as program code in C++, Python, and TensorFlow, with modules for interaction with a speaking user's voice, tables of objects the code would need to recognize, rules for recognition, rules of behavior, and now, rules of morality and ethics. Oh, and of course, to be able to recode itself, the system would need deep knowledge of the programming languages the team had coded it in. She hadn't thought of the system as needing a robotics interface, and when she reread the DARPA contest rules, she found no mention of the system needing an interface to a robot. But she was sure this was DARPA's oversight and the winning team would include this capability.

Early the next morning, her cellphone buzzed.

"Sashakovich."

"Hello. My name is Bertrand Rackal. I'm a finance major

in my last semester at the "B" school. I saw your recruitment advisory, and I'm interested. Is the position still available?"

"Yes. When are you available to meet?"

"Anytime today. Where and when?"

She scheduled him for eleven in the morning at the Nanoscale Science and Engineering building.

As she terminated the call, her cell buzzed again. It was another student from the MBA program.

By the time her morning ended, she had received six calls for her finance position and two for her human resources position. Her entire day was booked with appointments.

As her evening ended, she'd filled both open positions. Exhausted, she almost staggered home.

* * *

After dinner, she called a meeting of her cofounders at her apartment for the next morning. By ten a.m., cofounders started knocking on her door.

The five of them sat around the kitchen and living room amid the mess that she didn't have time to straighten from the living room. Ann and Dave Nordman sat on chairs at the kitchen table. Bertrand Rackal, the new finance lead, sat on the couch, along with Ken Simon, the new human resources lead, but Samantha Trout chose to sit on the floor with her back against the wall. Ann had brewed a few pots of coffee, and now, everyone held a filled cup.

Ann said, "I've revised the the DARPA contest application I'd submitted to include all your names. So now, we'll need to be all over this project at least half the hours of every day. It's a given that our studies will suffer. And there's nothing to be done for that. Each of you has your assignments listed in the emails I sent each of you earlier this evening. The dates are not negotiable, since the deadlines were set by DARPA. If we miss even one of them, we'll fail. So, if you foresee trouble, contact me. I'll find the additional manpower when you request it. Somehow."

The others all nodded. Each team member's email listed their first assignment as recruiting the talent they would need to manage the objectives within their own discipline.

Ann looked at each face to see if they were on board. "My first assignment for myself is to craft the executive summary of a business plan for this startup. It's due at DARPA the day after tomorrow. I'll get a draft done before tomorrow afternoon and send it via email to each of you. Please read it thoroughly and reply with any changes you feel necessary. Before I email the final to DARPA, I'll send you a 'final draft' and I expect you to either accept it or suggest changes before DARPA sees it. Okay?"

Again, everyone either nodded or gave a thumbs-up. They all turned toward the sound of the front door as it opened. Laura entered, and Ann pointed to her team members. Laura nodded. Ann said to her team, "This is Laura Hunter, my roommate. Laura, give us a few minutes and I'll clean up the room."

Once again, Laura nodded. "Hello, everyone."

Only Dave smiled back as Laura disappeared into the bedroom.

Then Ann asked each for their comments on the due dates. No one had any objections to them, and Ann ended the meeting.

When they had gone, Ann sat at the desk in the living room

and set to work, writing the draft of the executive summary. At this stage of the contest, no team had offices, a prototype, a prototype design, or even an executive summary of a business plan. She expected each of the teams' executive summaries would be similar, since most of the material would come directly from DARPA's own description of the contest. Although it was at the center of her mind, she made no mention of the "morality module" she wanted her team to code into their AI entry.

She worked until noon, then left her apartment for a scheduled class. When she dropped by the cafeteria for coffee and a sandwich, she saw a news story on the large-screen television. Some Chinese scientists were claiming they had moved a small amount of inanimate matter from earth to a satellite a few years ago, using what they described as a "matter transporter." Today's story claimed that they tried to move living matter—a mouse—but failed. However, the report claimed they also successfully moved over two hundred kilos of inanimate matter from earth to their satellite. The story did not mention whether the Chinese could move that matter from the satellite back to earth.

Ann realized the Chinese might soon be capable of transporting a robot army instantaneously from one locale on Earth to another. The thought left her stunned and shivering.

She wondered if she should mention these events in her executive summary.

She rewrote the executive summary to include the news item—the capability of transporting matter from one place to another without actual travel—as one of her business plan's mission objectives. She sent this to her team.

After each member of her team had approved the executive summary the next day, she sent it off to DARPA. While she was viewing the subpage for the contest, she read the statuses of the other teams in the competition.

Her team was on track with the others.

* * *

Major Zhou read the report on screen and nodded. "This looks good. The tech's concept has been proven and now we need to expand it. How soon can you show me the movement of a three-hundred-pound object?"

The captain standing at attention in front of him tried not to shrug. "Three months?" he ventured.

Zhou shook his head. "You have two weeks. Go now,"

He watched the captain leave and close the door to his office. *It will take at least three months before we can move a single, fully equipped robot soldier from one destination to another*, he estimated. *And from what the general told me, our own development of AI soldiers could take nearly a year. But soon, we can transport Russian robot soldiers to our research facility and simply copy the tech before the Russians have a chance to respond. Then our 3D printing facility can produce soldiers at a rate of six hundred a day. Yes. The next war will be interesting*. Zhou smiled with pride.

* * *

William Wing paced the small hotel room in Singapore. He turned to his wife, Betsy Brown, and shook his head. "Well, Butterfly, there's good news and bad news."

She rolled her eyes. "It's all bad news, little Wing. We have to leave the country right now. I think we may only have a matter of hours before they figure out who just stole their files and where we are."

He shrugged. "Let's just send the files on to Avram, then we can pack and leave."

She shook her head. "No. If they can track us, and if we send the files to Avram, they'll be able to track him too. Let's run now. We can send them to him when we get where we're going. By the way, where is that? Won't they be able to track us wherever we go?"

"You're right." He began throwing everything they both had in the hotel room into their two suitcases. "Either Manhattan, because then we can deliver the files personally by hand, or Beijing, since they also want the files."

"What about Moscow? Won't it be the last place they'd look for us? After all, we hacked the files from the SVR."

William stood stock-still while he thought. "Moscow?" He shook his head. "Too dangerous." Then he smiled. "Another thought. Maybe Tel Aviv would be the best. After all, the Mossad is our client."

Betsy laughed. "Yes. Now let's get out of here." She grabbed the gray suitcase.

William took the black suitcase and they headed together toward the hotel room door.

As they waited for the elevator, William wondered what the Mossad would do with Moscow's design documents for an AI-driven robot.

CHAPTER 8

Ann Sashakovich's apartment,
#211, 3950 Louis Road, Palo Alto, CA

September 7, 10:36 a.m.

The next morning, Ann's team met at her apartment for the second time to discuss their revisions, if any, to their staffing requirements and the obstacles they expected to encounter filling them. Once again, they were powered by an abundance of coffee.

Since Stanford was home to eight of the seventy-three DARPA contest teams, each person on Ann's team admitted vocally that the competition for staff candidates would be stiff. Samantha was the only one who shrugged, saying "no problem for me."

When Nordman asked her why she was so sure, Samantha responded, "Because we only have one customer, and that one is DARPA. Duh!"

Ann watched their interchange and wondered if Dave and Sam might not work together well. She asked the group, "Any other concerns?"

Nordman said, "I don't know how many programmers I'll need. But a lot, for sure. Maybe twenty, maybe fifty."

Bertrand and Ken nodded.

Bert said, "We'll be doing a lot of recruiting. What are we offering them to work on this? Just student credit? If it's cash, then I'll need to budget for it. And if it's cash, where will the money come from? Stanford might have something to say about this, so I'll have to meet with their director for student projects."

Ken Simon added, "I'll need to interview every one of your finalist candidates and set up records for them. The university has some guidelines and some rules about adding staff to student projects. I don't know how long this will take. How many candidates will you see to end up with thirty programmers?"

Dave said, "So far, the Stanford Student Projects Office has sent me two students, and both were too junior to be usable. I've approached nearly fifty of my classmates. Some weren't interested at all. Several have already signed up with other teams. Some claimed to have been offered cash salaries or stock to join one or another team. As a result, I've only signed three programmers to date, all for student credit and no cash. But, I'm guessing that it could take as long as—"

Ann interrupted, "Look, you three should do this together and then report back to me."

Bert and Ken's faces swiveled away from Dave's and toward Ann. All three shrugged.

Ann ended the meeting at noon, feeling defeated, and dragged herself to the kitchen for lunch and more coffee. Lots more coffee.

That afternoon, she walked to the library to complete research for one of her other courses. She passed by a crowd watching one of the large-screen monitors, which showed a chess tournament in progress between two computers, referred to by the announcer as "thinking machines."

The actual location for the match was in the library, and not far from where she stood. She jogged to the conference room of the library where she saw an enormous crowd of students.

Once the match started, it took less than a second between each machine's moves and the contest was over in under a minute. The winning machine belonged to one of the megacorps with its headquarters in Silicon Valley.

After it ended, Ann watched several chess experts on the television screen as they examined the moves and discussed the strategies of the machines.

She saw the programmers for the winning machine milling around the stage and followed two of them as they left.

One of the team members had a worried look on her face. She said to the person Ann thought was their team leader, "Our machine cheated."

The team leader nodded. "I saw it too. Check the code. Someone must have altered it. Were we hacked?"

The woman shook her head. "I scanned the code right after our machine moved two times in a single cycle. We weren't hacked. Our machine just did that on its own. But that wasn't all. It moved its queen off the diagonal by one row."

The team leader's jaw dropped. "Not possible."

Ann followed the woman and approached after her conversation with the team leader ended. She tapped the woman's shoulder. "How did you code this?"

The programmer shrugged. "Can't tell you much. We all signed NDAs. But I can tell you that each of us is working for Chesteronix. We all had a different idea, so we broke into competing teams." The programmer indicated the team leader.

"Carter's team had the most workable ideas, so we all folded back into his team. Took us almost a year, working full time."

Ann asked, "How many total employees?"

The programmer shrugged. "Well, that's the thing. It was expensive to complete this project. At peak, we had sixteen product designers, eighty system analysts, and nearly two hundred programmers. All our admin and facilities costs were fronted by Chesteronix's parent company. If we'd been a startup, that would have been at least fifteen additional employees. If we were a startup, the funding the effort would have taken at least two, maybe three venture capital rounds."

Ann's eyes bulged. "Wow. What's your next project?"

The woman replied, "A group of us are competing in the DARPA challenge."

Ann found herself unsurprised.

After Ann completed working on her class assignment, she returned to her apartment, worrying that her team's chances of winning were slim, at best. She turned on the evening news and watched the newscaster report on the chess match.

She felt her gut churning. She thought about quitting the DARPA contest.

CHAPTER 9

Ann Sashakovich's apartment,
#211, 3950 Louis Road, Palo Alto, CA

September 7, 6:18 p.m.

It was evening when Laura returned to the apartment.

Ann stopped humming a blues tune and watched Laura pass through the front door. Laura smelled the aroma of the spaghetti sauce Ann was cooking for dinner. Despite sniffing her favorite food, Laura frowned.

Ann wondered what was making Laura seem unhappy. "What's up? Bad day?"

Laura looked like she was about to burst into tears. "I'm taking a course in Gestalt psychology, hoping to work that into my degree."

Ann remembered that Laura had been majoring in modern and contemporary art restoration.

Laura said, "But, I'm finding that a lot of the Gestalt writings by Kurt Lewin and Wolfgang Koehler are confusing. The translations from German to English for Koehler are unreadable. Can I borrow you for a few minutes? I need help with the paper that's due tomorrow."

Ann didn't understand German and wondered what value

she could bring to solving Laura's problem. But she shrugged and said, "Sure." She motioned to the couch and turned off the burners on the stove.

Laura told her, "The Gestalt School sees the human mind as working in patterns to analyze problems and solve them. Their theories have art as the centerpiece of human cognition. For example, Dali's 'Slave Market with the Disappearing Bust of Voltaire.'" She showed Ann a color photo of the painting. As Ann examined the image, the head of Voltaire appeared and then disappeared into the construction of a building's archway.

Ann continued marveling at the construction of the scene in the Dali painting. She wondered if creating or analyzing a work like this would be a good test for an artificial intelligence? Then she was struck with the thought that Laura was already studying how humans reacted to Gestalt scenes. She decided Laura might be a good resource. "Laura, would you like a job working for stock shares in a startup? I'd like you to work with me on something called the Turing test. Alan Turing had been a computer engineer during World War Two. His test proposed that if you were talking to the machine but couldn't see it, would you be able to tell if you were talking to a human or a computer?"

Laura shrugged. "Not what I expected from you. What would I have to do?"

Ann smiled. "I think that just having you examining what we produce might have some benefit. How about it?"

Laura nodded. "Let me think about it for a bit. Could you help me with my paper?"

Ann nodded. "Sure." But she wondered if Laura would really spend a bit of time thinking about the offer.

* * *

In one of the lower floors of the building across the street from the Lubianka, the director of the Russian Republic's foreign intelligence service, the SVR, stopped eating his lunch as one of his associates knocked on the heavy wood door to his office. "What?" He looked at his associate, while puffing out his cheeks to accentuate his eyebrows.

"Director, I have just been informed that hackers have stolen files from the Committee for Robotic Research in Saint Petersburg."

"What was stolen?"

"Seven files, all plans for unit models of the robotic army. Four of them are our production models."

The director frowned. "Do you have any idea of who the hackers were?"

The associate nodded. "We know these two, a married couple. Their hack is nearly identical to several previous hacks traced to them. We have been tracking them for nearly three years. We don't have physical descriptions. Just the code they used to hack into our servers. One is Chinese and the other is American. This last hack left us new clues, and we're trying now to fit their hacks to their names. I'll be able to update you with their names and physical descriptions in a few hours."

The director nodded back. "Alert one of our assassination teams. Trace their whereabouts and tell me when we're ready to send the team." He leaned back in his chair. *Someone will get hurt when I inform the president.* He sighed.

* * *

Glen Sarkov sat in the classroom's back row of seats, not really paying attention to the lecture on robotics. The professor stopped speaking and handed back their papers, now graded. Glen expressed surprise and a little bit of frustration as he saw he'd received only a B- for his work. He smothered a curse and rose from his desk. He had twenty minutes to reach his next class. As he left the classroom, his cell buzzed. In the hallway, he pulled the cell from his pocket and saw that the name of the caller was blocked.

He answered anyway. "Sarkov."

"Glen Sarkov, you do not know who I am. I am a government official from Russia, where you were born. We need to meet. Russia has business with you."

"Go to hell. I'm not Russian any longer."

"No matter. I'm sending you a short video. After you see it, call me at the number I'm including in the email."

The caller terminated the call. Seconds later, his phone chimed with receipt of an email. Glen downloaded and watched. He saw his mother, standing in the doorway of their home in Fort Lauderdale, Florida, talking to whomever had recorded the video. His mother said into the camera, "Yes. Glen is at Stanford. I'm so proud of him." Then, as she smiled, the video ended.

So, the Russians want me to know they know where mom lives. He punched in the number embedded in the email's text. He had an idea they'd want copies of his AI plans and, when completed, their AI code. *But, why? From what I've seen on the news, their AI designs are well beyond what my team has produced. And so far, there's almost nothing to show for our work.* Glen shook his head in confusion.

CHAPTER 10

Ann Sashakovich's apartment,
#211, 3950 Louis Road, Palo Alto, CA

September 8, 8:42 a.m.

Laura sat in a chair in the apartment's kitchen. From just after dawn until now, she had read and reread Ann's first draft of the entire business plan several times. She thought, *I'm no use to Ann*, as she considered the plan and concluded her own experience was inadequate to deal a judgment on Ann's project, or even on the plan itself. *But, Ann's my roommate and she's been a friend to me when I really needed one*. She opened the plan to its first page and began reading it again. But ten more minutes left her with a lingering doubt and she felt torn. Then she thought about the geeky looking team member she'd seen at the meeting Ann held at the apartment. She felt herself smiling. He looked cute.

Her next class was to start in under an hour, so she grabbed her jacket and her notebook computer in its case, and set off toward campus. As she walked down University Avenue, she found her attention drifting back to Ann's plan. She thought more about AI than the traffic that could hurt her at each of the intersections. When she crossed west at Emerson Street, a car's horn brought her back to awareness of the real world. She nodded to the driver and stepped back onto the curb, where she took a deep breath. *Be here, now.*

She bought a spring roll at Rangoon Ruby and bit off a piece as she walked to her first afternoon class that day, held in one of the temporary classrooms among the pines and oaks.

She sat at a seat in the back of the small seminar room with the contents of Ann's business plans cycling endlessly through her mind. The professor walked into the room to the lectern and she tried to pay attention to him as he spoke, but time passed without his words sinking in. When the class ended, her notes page was blank but she had started to understand some of the AI concepts in Ann's plan. When she unlocked the door to their apartment, she sat in the living room and researched the meaning behind the concepts that still confused her. One-by-one, she began to have a clear picture of how AI worked.

While she and Ann ate dinner in the kitchen of their apartment, Laura said, "Ann, I've been thinking about your AI project all day. Do you really believe it's possible to build a machine that can think like a human?"

Ann shrugged. "Maybe. Probably. But the entire idea is to mimic human cognition. Not to re-create it. Big difference."

Laura said, "Well, that's confusing. What would this machine be able to do?"

Ann says, "Lots, and mostly things humans do poorly or don't want to do for themselves. First and foremost, the AI must be able to pass the Turing test I told you about."

Laura remained silent. Then she nodded. "Okay. I think I get it."

* * *

Ann knew that just the programming of an AI would be an enormous task. But feeding facts into the machine to complete the database that could get it to generate decisions would be close to impossible. *I'm sure if we try, we'll fail.* She wondered how to get Laura to understand this.

Ann remembered watching movies and television series with AI as primary characters.

After dinner, she said, "There's a movie we could watch that might give you a better feel for what I now think of AI. When I was younger, I saw AI as an achievable dream that could be a boon to humanity. But since I started working on the DARPA contest, I've grown increasingly fearful of it. Sort of like I feel about the Shelly book, *Frankenstein*." She used Netflix to stream *Ex Machina*, a low-budget movie starring Oscar Isaac.

She watched Laura's reactions as the movie played out. Too late, she realized that Laura found the movie very disturbing. Her roommate seemed riveted to the television, her face muscles so tense that her face was pale. Ann asked, "You okay?"

Laura replied, "No. But don't turn this off."

The next morning, she found Laura hunched over her notebook computer at the kitchen table, crying. When Ann approached, Laura said, "Don't!" and ran to the bathroom.

Ann peered at the screen of Laura's notebook. On it was the Wikipedia entry for the plot of *Ex Machina*:

In the movie, a programmer named Caleb Smith, who works for the dominant search engine company

Blue Book, wins an office contest for a one-week visit to the luxurious, isolated home of the CEO, Nathan Bateman. The only other person there is Nathan's servant Kyoko, who, according to Nathan, does not speak English. Nathan has built a humanoid robot named Ava with artificial intelligence. Ava has already passed a simple Turing test; Nathan wants Caleb to judge whether Ava is genuinely capable of thought and consciousness, and whether he can relate to Ava despite knowing she is artificial...

The description of the movie went on with more summary.

Ann waited for Laura to open the bathroom door. When at last she did, Ann said, "I'm sorry. I hadn't any idea the movie would affect you that way."

Laura shook her head. "It wasn't the movie. It was the prospect of this happening in real life. If the DARPA contest is successful, someday we'll all have to live side-by-side with these things, not knowing whether they're really human flesh and blood or soulless machines."

Once again Ann pondered whether what she and her team's cofounders were doing was good or evil.

* * *

The terminal at Ben Gurion International Airport was so crowded that William thought it felt like a traffic jam in rush-hour Manhattan. He followed Betsy from the customs line to the luggage return. While they waited for their suitcases, he thought carefully about their next step. "We should take a taxi to Herzliya. I can contact Avram to see if he can get us in to see someone at the Mossad."

Betsy nodded. "Yeah. But what if he can't help us?"

"One problem at a time." He drew his cellphone from his pocket and punched in Avram's number.

"Shimmel here, but I'm out right now. You know what to do."

"It's Wing. Call me back ASAP. We have a problem and an opportunity for you. Avram, we need your help."

They left the terminal and found the end of a very long taxi line. William's head swiveled to see if they were being followed.

Betsy saw this and her mouth opened wide. "Willy, stop. If they haven't found us yet, you're making it easier for them."

William nodded, but his head kept turning, albeit less frequently.

* * *

Glen Sarkov had become increasingly wary since his conversation with the Russian. He used the countersurveillance techniques he'd learned from his mother when they prepared to flee from Russia. He watched the reflections in windows as he walked to ensure he wasn't being followed.

He walked a surveillance detection route, an SDR, doubling back unexpectedly to see if anyone he saw was someone he'd seen previously.

He suspected his skills weren't up to the task. *Paranoia. I'm becoming paranoid!*

His first class was a seminar at 7:30 in the morning. The streets were relatively quiet and empty at this time. As he crossed University Avenue toward his classes on the Stanford main campus, a gray van pulled to the curb and three men exited its side door. Before he could react, they grabbed him in a rush and placed a cloth over his nose. He felt the effect of some drug immobilize him as the men pulled him into the van. His consciousness swirled away.

CHAPTER 11

Stanford University Cafeteria,
Stanford University, CA

September 8, 1:12 p.m.

As the end of her morning classes approached, Ann received a text from Dave Nordman requesting a face-to-face meeting. Ann immediately thought, *shit! He's going to quit.*

But when she arrived at the cafeteria, Dave smiled and pulled out a chair for her at the table he'd secured. He almost tripped over the chair, and muttered a curse. They sat in a corner of the cafeteria almost totally unoccupied.

He removed a printed Excel spreadsheet containing his staffing plan. She examined the rows and columns. "So, I see you've done concrete estimates of your staffing requirements. This shows that in order to complete the project on schedule, you'll require nearly fifty programmers in the early stages of development. Is that right? It's a lot more staffing than you estimated earlier."

Dave shrugged. "But that's what I'll need to meet our deadline."

Ann felt disappointed, even though she'd foreseen this obstacle. She took a deep breath.

Dave tapped her sleeve. "There's bad news and there's awful news. The bad news is the total staffing required. The awful news is most of them—probably all of them—will have to be paid, even if it's at substandard wages with stock options to soften the blow. Stanford isn't giving us nearly enough to cover this. You'll need a large funding round before they could even begin. And, you have to do that now, and fast. Get us investors and give them board seats."

Ann shrugged. Another problem to deal with. One that might easily end her team's ability to produce a viable product.

Dave said, "One more thing, unrelated to everything with our team. Your roommate, Laura. Would it be okay with you if I asked her out on a date?"

Ann suddenly realized that something had happened during the meeting that she had failed to notice. "Uh, well. Sure. I don't run her life. Go ahead if you want to."

And with that, Dave shrugged and rose from the table. "I got class now. See ya later."

She watched him rush through the cafeteria doors. Instead of feeling impending defeat, Ann found herself feeling rage now that she knew she'd be forced to face yet another obstacle. She opened her notebook and reviewed the rules for the DARPA competition. What she found there increased her anger:

> No team shall use venture capital, a long-term loan, or an offering of public stock (either IPO, ICO, or a secondary public offering) to fund the team in this contest.

The rules didn't mention angel funding. She thought about

this. Silicon Valley was filled with angels. Tech people who'd become rich from investing in pre-IPO projects, mostly from their own startups. She'd need to assemble a list and network these people immediately.

She started by Googling "Silicon Valley angel investors." She found a few entries that appeared promising:

- Band of Angels, at https://www.bandangels.com
- Angel Investing Network, at https://www.angelinvestmentnetwork.us/
- Silicon Valley Angel Investors, AngelList, at https://angel.co/silicon-valley/investors
- US Angel Investors, Silicon Valley and San Francisco Bay Area, at angelinvestors.com/
- SV Angel, at https://svangel.com/

She opened the webpage for one of the sites and scanned each of the member bios. She thought, *this looks like a formidable but interesting bunch of rich nerds*. She even took notes. She wrote a thirty-second "elevator pitch" and was about to launch her first cold call when her cell buzzed. "Mom? I'm a bit busy now. Can I call you back?"

"Give your mother a little bit of respect. I'm just asking for a minute or two, honey."

Ann realized she was being nasty. "Sure. How are you and dad?"

"We're each busy with work. Jon hired us to work for him at the United Nations Paramilitary Force. But I called to find out what you're up to. When we last spoke, you were about to form a team to enter the DARPA contest. How's it going?"

She frowned. "I'm worried more about what happens if I succeed than what happens if I fail."

"Interesting. I think you've grown up at last."

"Anyway, I remember you were an angel investor with the NYU Angel Group, so there's not much you don't already know. But, one thing I need to ask you. Do you still know other angels? It looks like I'll need a round of funding for the DARPA contest and they'll only let me accept angel investors."

"So, you did enter. I was going to ask you about that. Well, I could just fund your business myself. How much do you need?"

Ann thought about her mom's easy attitude about money. And, yes, it was true mom was rich beyond any need for money. She'd long ago hacked billions of dollars from an illegal US government program to fund terrorists and offer politicians an excuse to tighten immigration restrictions. But then she remembered Cassie's last adventure as an angel investor. "I don't think that's a good idea. The last time you put a heap of cash into a startup was GrayNet. Remember how that turned out? You almost died. No, mom. There might be unintended consequences with the DARPA contest. So, no, I won't use you as an investor."

She could almost hear Cassie frown. "Yes, I remember. You're right. But, I don't know any other angels anymore. I've been out of that loop for almost five years. What I can do is introduce you to the professor who runs NYU's Stern Graduate Business School's Angel Club."

Ann smiled. "Please do that."

"Okay. Ann, we miss you. When can you visit?"

Ann thought about the tight time constraints of the DARPA contest. "Maybe in a few weeks."

"Okay, but I want a commitment. When? Give me dates."

Ann pulled her schedule up on her notebook using one hand while the other hand held her cell. "I can make a three-day weekend in mid-October. No classes on Columbus Day and that's a Monday. Okay?"

"Thanks, honey. I promise you a feast and some company. Not just me and Lee. So now, you absolutely have to come. No cancellations allowed."

Ann agreed and ended their conversation. She would now need to work even harder to make space for the time lost traveling home and back, plus part of the weekend with her family. *I think this contest just might be the death of me.*

CHAPTER 12

**Ann Sashakovich's apartment,
#211, 3950 Louis Road, Palo Alto, CA**

September 21, 10:21 p.m.

The next two weeks passed Ann at a furious pace. Papers, exams and her nearly nonexistent social life left her feeling exhausted and frustrated. On a weekend night, Ann returned to her Palo Alto apartment after a long visit to the library, hunting down books for her next set of assignments. She tried to be silent as she walked into her small bedroom. She could hear Laura snoring.

Ann undressed and got into her bed. She pulled the covers to her chin, exhausted from the pace of studying, exams and papers, and the DARPA contest. She was asleep and dreaming, but not at peace.

She dreamed once more about Joshua's murder and her own rape, but this time she felt herself suffer through to the end and only the buzzing alarm on her cell ended the torture she'd felt when it had really happened seven years ago. Barely awake, she tried without success to shake the remnants of fear from her bones.

She washed and dressed, then found Laura in the kitchen pouring them each a cup of black coffee.

Ann sat next to her roommate in the kitchen, sipping,

Laura handed Ann a set of stapled pages. "It's my first draft of the midterm paper for the psychology course. Please, please do me a favor and read it. I need to know if a non-psychology major can understand what I'm arguing. I reviewed figure-ground relationships within the human brain. Specifically, which neural clusters trigger when someone sees the reversal of a visual relationship."

Ann nodded. "I'll read this today and get back to you on it tonight." She stuffed the paper into her bookbag and left for her early morning class.

That evening, after she'd read through the twelve pages and sat silent in thought, she waited until Laura returned to their apartment. "Hey Laura."

"Hey yourself. Did you read my paper?"

"Yeah. Well, I think the paper is brilliant. What else do you know about brain chemistry and physics?"

"As I told you last year, I'm finding art history to be frustrating. Don't think I'll ever achieve anything there. So, I changed my major to neuropsychology. Now I'm learning all I can about the chemistry of the brain. And I'm also taking a physics course, but I'm only just into that one. I need to know how people develop their mindset. I know my father sacrificed his freedom to give me a chance at being free. Why did I murder my mother? Why did he go to prison so I wouldn't have to? I need answers, and Stanford offers me the possibility of helping others if I'm able to help myself."

Ann was sure that Laura could add something she needed

for her startup team, but she didn't know if there was any way she could convince her roommate of this.

* * *

Glen sat in the old stuffed armchair of his apartment, considering his next move. During the half-day they'd held him captive, it had become clear that what the Russian president had claimed about his robot army's readiness was empty publicity. They had nothing that worked. Glen had come to believe that Russia needed to get the plans held by everyone else to see if the other countries had more advanced AI that they could copy.

To get the Russians to release him from their black site and stop threatening his mother, he'd agreed to spy on all the DARPA teams, especially his own, and report their status back to the Russians by using a series of burner phones they'd given him. But the only other team for him to possibly gather intel on was Ann's. And this was only if he could regain her trust. He'd already disappointed her, but he was sure this would breach their relationship and bust it unrecoverably apart. From last year, he'd learned her user ID at school, but he didn't know her current password. Knowing that she was a world-class hacker meant she would have multiple layers of additional security, so it wasn't even worth trying to hack her. He already knew she would never trust him again.

Glen decided it would be much easier to hack one of her team members. He logged into the DARPA contest and found the listing of the contest teams. She had six people on her team, all their names listed right under hers. He recognized three of them. Laura Hunter, Samantha Trout, and Dave

Nordman. Both women didn't like Glen: Laura because Glen had dumped her roommate, Ann, and Samantha because Sam had dumped him. He decided to poach Sam for his own team using a stock-option offer, but that might take too much time to set up.

He was sure that Dave Nordman wouldn't remember that Glen was in one of his classes. That would be the easiest path for him to discover what Ann's team had accomplished. He logged out and began devising a plan.

* * *

William and Betsy sat across from Samuel Meyer, the current director of the Mossad. The office, on the top floor of a squat building in Herzliya, was unnamed on its exterior, and William and Betsy had been told to enter through its underground garage. They had been kept waiting for a long time, and after surrendering their cellphones and wristwatches, they only knew it was afternoon from the light streaming into Meyer's corner office.

"I've been told you might know something of value," Meyer said to them.

William took off his right shoe and twisted its heel to the right. A thumb-drive dropped into his hand. He set it on the director's desk. "Plans for the Russian military robots."

Meyer picked up the drive as if it were dangerous. He pushed a button on his landline. "Michael, come here now. I have something for you."

Michael Drapoff, a tall, slim man with graying temples, smiled at the two visitors. "Hey, guys. It's been a long time."

William and Betsy both smiled back and rose. William

and Michael shook hands, and Betsy reached out and hugged Michael.

"How can I help, boss?"

Meyer handed Michael the thumb-drive. "Be sure to use an air-gapped quarantined machine. If it's safe, take a look at its contents. I'll need to know if it's useful."

Drapoff nodded and disappeared.

Meyer looked at his wristwatch. "I have another meeting to attend. I'll need you to stay for a while, until we know what you've brought us. Please follow me." He rose and led them from his office to an interrogation room containing one table with heavy steel rings to secure prisoners and several chairs. He pointed to the chairs. "Please sit. You'll be here for a while, unattended and able to relax."

William thought, *At least he didn't chain us to the table.* He nodded at Meyer, who tuned and walked out.

Betsy sat and frowned at William. As the door shut, she said, "No good deed goes unpunished."

PART 2

PART 2

CHAPTER 13

Ann Sashakovich's apartment,
#211, 3950 Louis Road, Palo Alto, CA

September 22, 8:13 a.m.

Cassie had complained about having to wait so long for Ann's visit. Ann was tired of hearing her mother complain, and as their mutual frustration grew, Ann decided to visit two weeks early.

Ann knew her long weekend with her parents would trap her on the East Coast. She purchased a ticket to fly home early Wednesday. But, she hadn't even packed yet.

After her last class, Ann rushed back to her apartment and tossed some of her clothing into her spinner suitcase.

Early the next morning, she passed through the security checkpoint and boarded the plane.

She had remained afraid of flying ever since two years ago, when the aircraft she was on to Washington was hacked. If Ann hadn't been able to hack the aircraft back from the CypherGhost, she would have been one of the over two hundred passengers that perished. For saving all their lives, Ann was arrested by the FBI for hacking just as soon as the aircraft landed.

She found her seat, swallowed a tranquilizer, and was soon asleep. She woke to the squeal of tires hitting a runway. She yawned and fetched her suitcase from the overhead storage. It was time to act her role as dutiful daughter.

Lee met her at the security exit. "Hey, sweetie. How was your flight?"

She yawned. "Five hours of chemically induced nightmares. Where's mom?"

"She had to start preparing dinner. A large dinner. Your uncle Misha and your grandfather Kiril will be at tomorrow's dinner. I think she's totally overwhelmed. She could use your help."

"Sure. Whatever. How are you?"

"Busy at work. I'm in the analysis section now. Working on Middle East scenarios."

They drove to the family compound in Lee's 1952 MG TD roadster. Ann felt the cold wind penetrating the ballooning ragtop. "How much is this antique worth?"

Lee shrugged. "Maybe eight thousand. But I just got it to run. So, no. I'm not selling it."

The car turned sharply into the compound's driveway and one of the guards waved at them, then opened the gate. Lee edged the car through the narrow gateway and coasted into the garage. He grabbed her suitcase and she followed him into the house.

Ann sniffed the air. She could smell what she knew was the result of a cook with very little talent. "Mom, can I help you with that?" She pointed to a large stock pot boiling on the stove.

Cassie turned and removed her oven mitt. She rushed across

the kitchen and hugged Ann. "Ah, the conquering heroine returns home. How I've missed you."

They smiled at each other. Ann picked up the oven mitt. "What should I be doing?"

Cassie seemed to study the kitchen. She turned off all the burners on the stove. "Nothing. We'll cook later. Tell me all about your semester."

"We completed staffing the AI project, but we're behind schedule and it's beginning to put us all in a bad mood. We're trying to get the prototype to work, but so far, no love. Dave tells me to be patient. My grades are okay, considering that I've spent almost half my available hours on the contest. And, now I see what Glen went through trying to run a team. God, it's hard work."

Cassie nodded. "Leading and managing are polar-opposite skills. Are you a leader or a manager? Few are good at both."

Ann shrugged. "Not really a leader. I seem to be able to manage, and most of my team is better at both than I am at either."

Cassie flashed a look of concern. "Pick one and find a mentor. That's my advice. But don't expect yourself to become effective without failure. Glen learned his lessons by taking his lumps. You might need to, too."

Ann shivered with the knowledge that running a team could be so painful. She had a lot to learn that her professors couldn't teach her.

Cassie had already set the table for dinner. Lee and Kiril walked in, talking about the roadster. Ann took a seat and poured wine for all four of them.

Kiril asked, "What have you learned this semester, little one?"

Ann told him about the AI contest.

Kiril asked, "Do you think AI is dangerous?"

"I'm not sure. I think if we encode a morality and ethics subroutine into the AI, it could be helpful, not a threat."

Lee passed a tray of vegetables to Ann. "Your mom took almost two hours prepping these."

Ann nodded and plucked a portion of string beans in garlic sauce from the tray. "Thanks."

Misha shook his head. "Russia will buy, not develop."

Lee said, "Misha, every country with ambitions of power is developing AI weapons. So, I believe you're right. AI is dangerous. Maybe Ann's plan to inject morality into their code might work. But when it takes the humanity out of killing, there's no way to control what the end product does. Robots will never have second thoughts about what they do."

Cassie stopped chewing a piece of Beef Wellington. "I've been thinking about this for nearly a month. My opinion is that it's too early to tell how AI will change the world. But, by the time we know, it'll be too late to change what we've done."

Ann thought about that for a while. She thought, *Cassie is right*.

* * *

It rained all morning during their long train trip to Manhattan. Cassie read Ann's business plan and offered her a critique. "It's good. Not great. You need to show your enthusiasm in every section of the plan, but especially in the executive summary. If that section doesn't engage your investor, they won't read any further. What you have here isn't compelling. The old saying is, 'Will the dogs eat the dogfood?' Yours won't."

Ann pulled the plan from Cassie's hands and read her executive summary. She sighed. "Mom, it's giving me shivers to think about the contest. It might not even be possible to create sentient AIs, given the current state of technology. The time constraints of the contest are like a brick wall and we're all running at light speed towards it. All I do every day is put out fires. Worst of all, I'm not convinced what I'm doing will be a boon to the world."

Cassie's face wrinkled in confusion. "If you don't believe in what you're selling, why are you trying to sell it? If you aren't a believer, you can't expect any potential investor to believe in it either."

Ann sat in her seat motionless, her mouth hanging open. She whispered, "Fuck." Then she picked her notebook computer from her backpack and opened the business plan file. Her fingers flew across the keyboard as Cassie watched.

Cassie read over her shoulder. She smiled. "Good. Very good."

It took two hours for the train to cross into New Jersey and another hour for it to chug into Newark. The orange sky was a sign of pollution, not sunset. The aroma of effluent petrochemical gasses seeped into their car and the two women shifted in discomfort. When at last the train entered the tunnel into Manhattan, Ann closed the lid on her notebook, hoping the work she'd done would help her find the investors she sorely needed.

They caught a taxi outside Penn Station and Ann stared at the new construction in Manhattan since she'd left the island six years ago. Washington Square was brown with fallen leaves and bare trees. She thought, *what a difference between the East Coast and the West Coast.* But, all the time they sat in their taxi, mired in the traffic, she found herself fearing her presentation. *I'm not really ready.* She found herself biting her fingernails.

They left the taxi at the corner of West 4th Street and LaGuardia Place. Cassie led them up the stairs to the Stern Business School's main building. Ann stopped in front of the circular windows that fronted the doorway. The building was a formidable fortress of granite, glass, and steel. She felt a sense of awe.

Cassie pointed to the revolving doors. "Come on. I'm glad I anticipated the heavy traffic. We're just a bit early. Maybe I can make a few introductions for you before it's time for your presentation." Ann watched as Cassie drew herself up to her full height and assumed a more confident pose.

She followed Cassie into the auditorium. It was only half filled, mostly with men, all wearing dark blue suits, white shirts, and dark, patterned neckties. She felt out-of-place and wanted to shrink away.

Cassie faced her and pointed to a tall, willowy blond. "There's Dr. Longstein. Come and I'll introduce you." She led Ann to the woman who seemed the essence of middle-aged elegance. Longstein wore a dark-blue pantsuit that seemed to match the exact color of the men's suits.

"Blanche, this is my daughter, Ann."

Dr. Longstein smiled at Ann. "Welcome, Ann. You'll be up fifth."

Cassie scanned the room and took Ann's hand. "I know three of the angels." She walked over to a man about Cassie's own age. "Steven, this is my daughter, Ann. She'll be present-ing an AI project today. Ann, this is Steven Goldman, one of the principals at Angel Vision."

Ann smiled and shook his extended hand. She tried to assume an attitude of confidence, but it felt false.

She watched the first four presenters as they went through their time on the podium. She saw the angels take notes on their cells. When it was her time, she plugged her notebook into the lectern's HDMI port and adjusted the height of the microphone so it was inches away from her face. "Good afternoon, angels. My name is Ann Sashakovich and I'm the daughter of Cassandra Sashakovich, one of your members. I'm CEO of a project, as yet unnamed and unincorporated, to produce the first sentient AI. Our product is aimed at the military, and our first milestone will be to win the DARPA Sentient AI contest, currently underway." She pointed to the screen, with an organization chart showing the photos and titles of each of her cofounders. "Each member of my team is a junior at Stanford University. So, I'll spend a few minutes going over our team and then I'd like to show you our plans to win this contest, which comes with much of the funding we'll need to bring the product to market." She opened the next slide...

* * *

Cassie and Ann stood on the platform in Penn Station, waiting for the train back to Washington, DC. Ann felt the heat wafting off the tracks, hoping it would distract her from the disappointment she felt from her performance at the Angel Club. She was haunted, remembering that during her presentation, she didn't see any of the angels take notes. She was sure that she'd failed.

When they took their seats, Cassie said, "Don't worry. I'm sure you'll get some interest."

Ann shrugged. "At least it was good practice." They heard her cellphone chime. "That was fast." Ann drew her cell from her pocket and opened the email app. She and Cassie read the note that had just arrived.

> Dear Ann,
> Thanks for your presentation this afternoon.
> Sorry, but it's not for us.
> Sincerely,
> Steven Goldman
> Principal, Angel Vision

Ann stared into her mother's eyes. "They're all going to send me notes like that one." She wiped her eyes.

Cassie nodded. "Perhaps. But don't give up hope yet."

And as the train pulled into Union Station, Ann received the last of the thirty-six emails from NYU's Angel Club. But this one was longer and had several attachments:

> Dear Ann,
> Thanks for your presentation this afternoon. We at
> Gorilla Startups are interested in having you present
> to our full board of directors meeting tomorrow, at
> 2 pm. If it's inconvenient for you to be present, we
> can arrange the presentation using Google Hangouts.
> Attached you will find some documents we'd like
> you to review and sign, and instructions for using
> Hangouts should you want to present to us that way.
> Sincerely,
> Arnold Bruce
> Partner, Gorilla Startups

Cassie hugged Ann. "So, I guess you'd better get started learning how to use Hangouts."

Ann's mouth hung open once again, but she smiled. "Wow. And, I've used Hangouts before, so no worry."

* * *

The next day, Ann smiled as she greeted her grandfather and her uncle at the door to the compound. Cassie ended up cooking some adequate courses, including Beef Wellington, home fries, cornbread stuffing, and a massive cherry cobbler. Ann drank too much Chardonnay, celebrating her Hangouts presentation to Gorilla Startups. She had answered the potential investors' questions with brutal honesty, and yet, just an hour after, they sent her an email containing an acceptance letter and more forms to review, sign, and mail back. When the evening ended, she slept in the bed she'd used while in high school. No nightmares.

* * *

As the airplane touched down at SFO two days later, Ann felt happy. *A full seed round. Don't know I managed that.* She couldn't wait to tell her cofounders at the next meeting, scheduled for tomorrow.

* * *

Dave Nordman sat in his dorm room, thinking. *What to do? What if she wants nothing to do with me? Oh, fuck me. I have to try*. He keyed the number he'd hacked from Laura Hunter's Facebook page into his cell. He heard it ring twice.

"Hello?"

"Laura, it's Dave Nordman. I work with your roommate Ann on the DARPA project."

"Yeah. I remember seeing you at Ann's meetings. Ann's in New York. She'll be home tomorrow."

"I'm not calling for Ann. I'd like to ask you out for dinner."

"Me?"

There was silence on the line that seemed to last forever. Dave thought, *this was a bad idea*. He was about to end the call when…

"So, Dave. Where do you want to take me?"

He swallowed, realizing his mouth was so dry that it was difficult to speak. His voice felt ragged as he said, "What kind of food do you like?"

"Surprise me. I'm free tomorrow night."

He felt a surge of fear. "Great. Can I pick you up at your place at seven?"

"Sure. I'll be waiting."

CHAPTER 14

Cecil H. Green Library,
557 Escondido Mall, Stanford University, CA

September 26, 8:09 a.m.

Dave Nordman sat at alone in one of the library's small conference rooms and stared at his wristwatch. He smiled at the thought of last night. Laura seemed to be easily entertained. He hoped she'd enjoyed the night as much as he had. Sure, there had only been a goodnight kiss at the end, but so what? He hoped for more.

Outside, the day was warm and bright, but the room's door had been closed before he arrived and it was chilly where he sat.

He expected his team leaders to arrive soon for their daily status update and his fingers tapped the oak table as he reran his agenda for the umpteenth time.

Gradually, the five data specialists and programmers arrived. He pointed to the chairs and they took the seats around him.

Each one he'd hired had a different discipline in IT. He looked at Harry Schofield and nodded. Harry managed a small team in database management. Harry pulled a few pages from his backpack. "We're on track, and on schedule. No problems."

Then Dave's gaze shifted to Gary McHahn. His group was composed of Python programmers. Gary merely nodded back. "Me too."

Stuart Ley smiled at Dave. Stuart's group consisted of C++ programmers. But then, Stuart looked away, a bad sign. Didn't people look away when they wanted to conceal something, or even worse, lie?

Sandra Elmont frowned at Dave. She headed her group of Tensor specialists. Sandra pulled a pen from her pocket and a pad from her attaché case. "I found a problem in the code Stuart is using to populate the database. Actually, three bugs." She ripped the first page of the pad off and handed it to Stuart.

Stuart read the page and his face turned red. "Crap. You could have sent this to me in an email instead of telling the entire team."

Sandra shrugged. "I just found them fifteen minutes ago."

Dave said, "Relax. Just fix the problem."

When Dave looked at Walter Graves, Walter merely shrugged. His group was systems analysis. Dave considered Walter the easiest one to manage. Walter was so easygoing. "No problems and we're also on schedule."

As the meeting ended, Dave thought that overall, they were on track to meet their schedules for producing their pieces of a functional prototype.

After he ended their brief meeting, Dave reported back to Ann via email, He included the first flowchart of the planned functions for the AI they intended to build. He also included a list of functions with a tiny bit of description:

Macro	Micro	Language
Input modules:	cam	Python
	Mic	Python
	Text and news docs	C++
Output:	Speech	C++
	Image recognition	Tensor
	Figure/Ground Understanding	Python
Processes:	Analysis	Systems Analysis
	Altering real reality	Tensor
	Feedback and adjustments	Systems Analysis
	Self-recoding and code optimization	JavaScript

He thought of adding two more columns, one for required hours and another for ETA, but he wasn't ready yet to wade through the hours of discussion and argument necessary to forge an agreement with each of his programmers and analysts. Dave pondered the language column of the chart for a long time. He wondered if the AI could really be taught to recode itself? If it could, it would save calendar days, maybe even calendar months of time. He set about researching how they could do this.

* * *

At her apartment while she dressed for her first class of the day, Ann heard Laura in the bathroom. The door opened. Seeing Laura's smile, Ann said, "You look happier than I've ever seen you."

"Yeah. I had my first date in months."

Ann remembered Dave asking about Laura. "Nordman?"

"How'd you know?"

Ann chuckled. "He asked me if he could take you to dinner. As if I was your mother!"

Laura cocked her head. "Really? I guess he really is geeky. But he made me feel happy."

"Well, good luck. He's bright and I think he has a good future ahead of him."

Laura literally danced back into the bedroom to get dressed.

Ann returned her attention to Dave's report and thought, *this might actually work.* She replied to Dave, *remember to place safeguards on the thoughts and behavior that your AI can develop. We need an "ethics" module.*

While she sipped a cup of coffee, Dave sent her back a text: *Well, duh!*

Ann's misgivings faded. She placed her notebook computer in her backpack and headed off to the apartment building's elevator. She felt happy about the team's potential and their progress, but still had nagging doubts about what the team's efforts would produce. *Can a morality module really fix the potential an AI has to harm humanity?*

CHAPTER 15

DARPA Headquarters,
Strategic Technology Office (STO),
675 North Randolph Street, Arlington, VA

September 30, 8:49 a.m.

Dr. Linda Beam parked her car in the DARPA parking structure and passed through the security gate of STO, DARPA's Strategic Technology Office. Just last week she had finally been promoted to DARPA project manager at age twenty-eight, the average age for her position. At five-foot six, she was also average height for female DARPA employees, and the average intelligence for her position, and, she thought, not especially attractive. *Average in every way.* The very thought of her averageness left her unhappy as she bought a cup of coffee and a doughnut in the lobby and took the elevator to the fifth floor.

After walking through the warren of cubicles and narrow pathways on her floor of the building, she found hers. A poster of Lake Como hung on the cubicle's fabric wall. It was a place she'd never been to and wasn't particularly interested in visiting, but the poster was vibrant and, she believed, capable of provoking visitors into believing she had non-average dreams.

Other than that, there was nothing to indicate her personality or what she wanted from her job or her life.

But this promotion might change her life. Tomorrow she would move from cubicle hell to a tiny office, one of the few perks of her promotion.

She sat at her desk watching the clock that would count down until the deadline for teams to apply for the AI Competition. *Under one minute now left.* As the seconds passed and the alarm on her watch buzzed, she sighed. *Finally. Let me see how much work I've gotten myself into. Ninety-two teams are enrolled. The first deadline is in two weeks, and then a string of them every few days until December 1, when the competition ends.*

She reviewed the completed team applications. *Thirty-two teams staffed by startup companies, fifty from universities, and ten from publicly held tech corps.* She examined the details for each team and guessed that only half would participate to the end and fewer than one-third would achieve any palpable result. Of the ninety-two entrants, she estimated sixteen might achieve a satisfactory result over the next two months.

Based on past contests, she thought, *I'll need four judges for about two months to judge the sixteen semifinalists.*

She wrote a memo to DARPA's STO management requesting staff time from four senior project managers.

* * *

Ann and Dave sat at the desk in his dorm room and stared at a summary of his team-leader status reports displayed on his notebook computer's screen.

Ann said, "I see the problem. Do you have any ideas about how to fix it?"

Dave shook his head. "Not yet. But there are a few work-around tactics that might help."

Ann nodded. "Like?"

"We could just comment out the ethics module until we can get it to work properly. Meanwhile, we can construct a list of situations that require ethical judgement and review the parameters of choices for each one. If we group them by similar characteristics, like severity, impact, or any other characteristic you can imagine, then we can come up with a set of general guidelines from which to form the rules."

"I guess that might be a start." But Ann wasn't sure how the process would work. "Let me think about this and get back to you later today."

Dave said, "Okay. But the hard part will be prioritizing which rule takes effect when there are two or more outcomes that have alternatives in conflict with each other. For example, a simple case is, suppose a runaway train is about to run into and kill five innocent people on the track, but you are in a position to act quickly and switch the train to another track, where only one person on the track would die. Would you do nothing and allow five to die, or actively steer the train to kill one innocent person? There are a whole set of similar cases, and some of them are quite complex."

Ann shuddered at the thought of having a machine make this type of judgement. "Who on your team will be handling the input for the tables?"

"That's up to us. We already have the Tensor tables ready to collect what we input. But as to the judgements, I haven't assigned anyone yet."

Ann reviewed the staff under Dave's management. She thought Sandra Elmont, the only woman on the tech team, might be a voice of empathetic reason, but then immediately realized this was her own preconception. "Let me think about this for a few days. How much time do I have?"

Dave shrugged. "Maybe a day. More likely a few hours. There's a ton of data we'll have to enter. So get back to me fast and I'll get it started. Oh, and I also have a general status report for you."

Ann rose and paced Dave's room. "Give it."

"Walter Graves's group has produced a final form of the systems flow chart," Dave said. "All the screens detailing the processing of the giant AI mind had been buried by the analysts below the overall flow chart. Walter is fixing that. The revised screens will be at the top level of the flow chart, making it easier to understand and debug. It might at first look way too complex, but it's complete and workable.

"Gary McHahn's group completed a prototype of the AI's functioning in Python. It looks like it might work, but McHahn reported there are several major bugs in the code, and they still need to be fixed. He estimates it might take a few days until his prelim work is complete." Dave stared at Ann until she nodded.

"Okay then. Stuart Ley's group has started on C++ programs to develop a settings module. When I attempted to run it, it worked perfectly. His status report says that their next step is to flesh out the data-entry module in JavaScript that records the settings for the AI into a final form. He claims it'll take about a week to complete. They plan to test both modules in tandem."

Dave paused just a moment before continuing. "Sandra

Elmont's Tensor specialists placed each piece of event code into a framework, but they are still missing the data segments. Elmont and Ley would need to fit their modules together and then test them. This will be the first time two of my groups have needed to work together." Ann nodded again.

"Then, there's Harry Schofield's database management group. Harry outlined the data dictionary and showed me a preliminary design for organizing the data population. When he's done that, Harry and Sandra will need to make sure their pieces work together, hand in glove."

Dave made a quick mental calculation. "I figure the entire process is about ten percent complete."

He walked to the whiteboard in his dorm room and drew a top-level system flowchart of the AI. He watched Ann study it.

She smiled. "Good work. Thanks."

* * *

After Ann left, Dave shook himself, *Why do I fear her? Is it because I report to her, or is it because she's my gatekeeper to Laura?* He sat and tried to relax himself, shaking out his hands. He needed to think about something else to clear his head. *What gender and what name for the AI? But maybe it's a bit early to name the AI.*

* * *

Michael Drapoff opened the door to the interrogation room. William and Betsy both looked up.

"We're vetted the data on the thumb-drive. Sorry it took so long. Looks like you've netted a gold mine. And, you're correct. The Russians will be hunting you. We'll need to hide you two in one of the safe houses we have in Tel Aviv. I'll take you now."

William shrugged. He took Betsy's hand and the three walked to the elevator. "How many guards?"

"We'll give you three to start off. We're also monitoring the Kremlin to see their reaction. They usually just kill anyone they think may be a problem, so if we see anything bad coming your way, we'll rush reinforcements to you."

Betsy stared incredulously at Michael. "Reaction? Like they're gonna fucking wanna buy us from you? Listen, Michael, they want us dead. We expected this, but we didn't think you'd need us for follow-up assignment where we are the bait."

Now, Michael shrugged. "Spies lie. We'll lie when they ask us to confirm. And they'll know it. You guys know how the game is played."

"To you, it may be a game, but for us, it's no game." Betsy cast her eyes at the floor of the moving elevator. "Fuck us."

The doors opened and Michael led them through the garage to a black SUV. There were three very large men waiting there. Now six, the group loaded into the SUV, with William and Betsy in the middle back seats.

William heard the engine fire, then watched through the dark tinted windows as the SUV left the garage and headed toward the highway. He thought, *Dicey. I wonder if the Russians stationed in Israel have received their orders to kill us just yet?*

* * *

Glen closed his notebook as his afternoon class ended. He

walked with the other students from the classroom. On his way down the stairs he saw Dave Nordman climbing the stairs. He'd seen Dave and Ann conversing before and had taken the time to research every one of Ann's team profiles. Glen smiled and caught Dave's attention. "Hi, Dave. I'm Glen. I'm sure Ann told you about me. How's the DARPA project coming along?"

Nordman didn't return the smile, but he moved out of the way of the traveling students. When Glen also moved out of the traffic, Dave shrugged. "The contest is a hell of a lot more work than I'd imagined. How did you do it last year and what made you believe it would be cool to try in again?"

"Last year, the startup was a new challenge. This year, none of the challenges was unexpected for us. Been there, done that, as they say. And remember Murphy's Law. For this contest, I think that law will hit us harder, because DARPA set all the deadlines." He pointed down the hall. "Want my advice?"

They walked into an empty classroom.

"First, tell me your team's status. Then I'll give you hints as to the obstacles on your horizon."

Dave wondered if he was about to agree to a nasty deal with a nasty enemy. "Really, now? Why would you want to help me?"

"Because I still feel bad about what happened between Ann and me last year. You know."

Dave nodded. *But can I believe anything Glen said? I might as well play along until I understand the parameters of this situation.* Then he suppressed a giggle as he realized this would be a version of the ethics module's decision-making for the AI his team was coding. *Life following art.*

CHAPTER 16

Ainsley/Sashakovich House,
220 Kirke Street, Chevy Chase, Maryland
September 30, 6:11 p.m.

Cassandra Sashakovich looked around the kitchen. She thought, *this house is too empty. Way too big for just two people.* But, the dining-room table where she and Lee sat was set for just the two of them.

She cut a slice of pork chop and chewed it while she thought about Lee's question. "Well, if we have to decide whether we trust the folks at DARPA, the answer right now would be to look at their past performance. Our government never treated me with fairness. And, they tried to kill both of us numerous times. The question would then become, how much is DARPA like the rest of government? After all, spies are trained in disseminating disinformation. Lies. When we were spies, we constantly lied. And when spies lie to elected officials, those officials lie to voters like us. I hate to see Ann playing with this monster."

Lee swallowed a sip of the cherry-colored Monterey County Pinot and shook his head. "I've worked with DARPA and my own experiences are mixed. They're one of the most honest of the Fed's agencies, but these days they seem to have grown ever more blatant about designing war tools. Of course, that's not what they tell us."

"So, then, what would happen to Ann's prospects for a normal life if her team successfully completes their DARPA contest entry? Will the Fed foreclose any other job alternatives for her? Will they force her to work for them?"

Lee nodded. "Yes, I think they might, especially if she wins. I don't trust either DARPA or Ann to make mature decisions. And we both know Ann doesn't trust authority figures. Even us. It would be better if we could spend a few months with her while she finishes the contest. But both of us have exhausted all our vacation and paid time off. If we take off time without pay, the government will become suspicious. So, we'll need a surrogate to watch her if that's what you agree we should do."

Cassie shrugged. She could see that Lee had already decided. "William and Betsy aren't available. Jon sent them out on assignment and they'll be gone for months. Who else is there to be a sounding board for her and act as a bodyguard if things start to go south?"

Lee sat in silent thought. "Sommers."

"But Jon lives in Manhattan, 2,500 miles away from Palo Alto and Ann. And Jon has a full-time job running the UN paramilitary force. Is it even possible for us to get him to do this for us?"

"Only one way to find out." Lee pulled his cellphone from his pocket and punched in a number. He turned on the phone's speaker.

"Sommers."

"It's Lee and Cassie. We need a favor. From you or someone you trust. We have an issue with Ann and need someone she trusts to be her bodyguard and mentor in California."

Sommers' laugh came through the speaker. "Ann trusts no one. Certainly not me. But she does owe me one and I can't tell you what it's for. This place is driving me crazy with diplomatic doublespeak. I need a vacation, and, oh yes, it looks like I've accumulated nearly two months. So right, then, I'll babysit your daughter."

Cassie smiled at Lee. "Thanks, Jon. Now we owe you one too."

After the conversation ended, Lee said, "We should speak with Ann right now. We'll need to ask her permission to do what Jon has just agreed to do. Let's make a plan."

Cassie nodded. "Deviousness is our best talent, love."

Suddenly, the overly spacious house didn't feel quite as big to Cassie.

* * *

William wasn't quite sure he'd heard what Michael Drapoff had just said. "You want us to do what?"

Michael repeated his plan more slowly. "I want you two to walk out from Mossad 's headquarters building through the front entrance and hail a taxi. Take it to the hotel we'll book for you. Then wait there. We'll have you under close surveillance."

Betsy's reaction was far more volatile. She shouted, "Absolutely not!"

Michael shrugged. "I expected you to say no. But, in order to make sure the Mossad's plan works, we'll need to effect this little charade."

William leaned forward in his chair in the safe house. "We've been here for a few days now, and you want us to simply walk out onto the street, alone, and see who catches us. The Russians will kill us, maybe interrogating us first, or maybe just driving by. The Chinese would interrogate and torture us. Either way, we'll die. Why the fuck would we want to do this?"

"William, we'll be with you every step of the way, and we'll stop it before it gets dangerous."

"You can't guarantee that you can save our lives." Betsy shook her head. "You're fucking batshit crazy."

Michael sighed. "Both the Russians and the Chinese are developing weaponized AIs, but we don't know how far along any of them are. There are multiple players, all of them holding their cards closely. If we can capture any of their operatives, we can get information from them using chemical interrogations. You would be heroes. And, we have new tech that uses an undetectable tracker and also channels what you see and hear directly back to us. A new version of Bug-Lok. We'll be less than fifty meters behind you. We'll have snipers riding the roofs of buses, keeping you in range. And, after you have delivered the message and they send it back to their handlers, we'll engage."

William looked at Betsy. She shrugged. William faced Michael. "So help me, Michael, if you let us die, we'll become golems and haunt you for the rest of your life."

Michael took a deep breath. "The state of Israel owes you a great debt."

Betsy said, "And you'd better pay it in cash."

* * *

Dave Nordman smiled at Glen. "Our team is close to achieving the prime objective. My guess is we'll be at the finish line before the week's end."

Glen felt a weakness in his entire body trunk. "Really?"

"Yeah. Listen, Glen, it's been nice, but I'll be late for my next class if I don't get going now." Dave waved once and descended the stairs.

Glen found a relatively empty corner of one of the snack rooms. He sat at a desk and sent a text to his Russian handler, containing details of the brief conversation he'd just had with Dave. Then Glen waited.

It took just a minute before he received the encrypted return message from his handler. Using the instructions he'd been given, he decrypted the reply. He bought a chocolate bar from the snack machine and sat back down to eat it. At least the chocolate tasted good, diverting his attention from the ugly task before him.

"Close to the prime objective." How could that be? But, that's what he'd told the Russians. Glen knew he needed some way to escape their influence, but with his mother under their constant observation, their threats still held currency with him.

He still couldn't believe he was doing this. He felt disgust with himself, and now the candy no longer tasted sweet.

* * *

Dave Nordman wasn't a pathological liar. But he knew when someone was trying too hard to glean secrets from him, and he knew how to lie. As he walked from Glen's apartment to his dorm room, he chuckled at his lie. In fact, Ann's team was lost among the groups. He didn't expect them to achieve anything close to a success. *All we'll get is credits toward our diplomas, but that's enough.*

He wondered if any of the teams would achieve success. Maybe the one from Google or the one from Microsoft. When he climbed the stairs to his floor in the dorm, he passed several students he knew and he nodded and smiled at them. After closing the door of his bedroom, he made a call. "Hi, Ann. It's Dave."

"Dave? What's up? Is there something I need to handle?"

"No. But I have something you might find interesting."

"Okay. What?"

"Your former beau, Glen, just tried to pump me regarding our status."

"He what?"

"You heard it right. Anyway, I told him we're really close to achieving a miracle."

"Why?"

"Come on, Ann. Relax. What difference would it make if I told him a lie?"

Ann was silent for a while. "Please, don't do that again."

"Okay. G'night."

Dave ended the call and chuckled. He imagined Glen worrying about how his team was about to lose the contest.

CHAPTER 17

**Stanford University Seminar Classroom,
Stanford University, CA**

October 1, 9:01 a.m.

Dave Nordman sat at the back of the class in the seat closest to the door. Every other seat in the class was taken, just as he'd hoped. Now, if he drifted into sleep during the lecture, perhaps no one would notice. As long as he didn't snore.

He had a clear view of the professor, the whiteboard, and all the students. Especially Ann. The professor seemed to be wrapping up the morning's lecture on the perils of Artificial Intelligence. The professor reminded them all that their midterm papers were due at the next class, and Dave watched as his note-taking dictation software typed the professor's reminder word-for-word into his notebook. He closed its lid and reached to the floor to retrieve his bookbag.

As he placed his computer in the bag and rose to leave for his next class, he saw Glen Sarkov walk over to Ann. Dave pulled his cellphone from his pocket and opened the video recorder app. He recorded Glen's voice and image, then stopped the app and pocketed his cell. He was sure there was enough content there for him to finish his self-assigned task.

Late that afternoon, he returned to his dorm room and used the recordings of Glen's voice to craft a complete vocabulary of Glen's speech patterns. He uploaded the vocabulary and the photos into the AI prototype. Then he used C++ to flesh out how the face muscles should move as the AI spoke.

He prompted the prototype's code within his notebook: "Speak to me."

The prototype replied, "Slooshly enturg Ratsmith." It sounded just like Sarkov. But more important, its face looked just like Sarkov.

Dave chuckled. *Damn! Won't Ann be surprised!*

Then he had second thoughts about showing her what it had taken less than an hour for him to complete. *What if she doesn't like it?*

He replayed the conversation he'd taped between Glen and Ann to decide whether his modification of the AI prototype would make her happy.

The recording had Glen asking Ann, "I'd like to have dinner with you. Can we meet later this evening?"

Ann had replied, "Glen, you and I both are leading teams competing in the DARPA contest. So, no. We're competitors now."

Dave realized she wouldn't be amused at his prank. He decided to delete the changes before anyone on the team saw them. But by the time he was able to reload the modules to modify their code, it was too late. Everyone on the team had seen and spoken with the prototype. Including Ann.

* * *

Arcady Kaslov faced the cryptographic telephone encoder and

smoothed his hair into something more presentable than his usual wide-spiked haircut. He pressed the connection button and waited for the telecommunications handshake.

He heard the brief click and saw the image of Director Ivan Tranovich, his handler in Moscow, several thousand miles away. "It's Kaslov. I sent you a video a few minutes ago. You can see for yourself, Director Tranovich. The prototype can speak."

"Yes, but it says nothing but garbage. It's not as advanced as your little spy says it is. Right now, the world believes we have the only sentient AI. And as you know, ours is a subterfuge and nothing more than garbage. If the Americans are closer to a breakthrough, we need to stop them. We must get there first."

Kaslov sighed. "What about the Chinese? They claim theirs is more advanced than the Americans'."

He saw the director's face flush. "We have another team working on that. Not your concern. You must handle the Americans. Stay focused. The Sashakovich team seems to be closer to its objective than any of the other teams."

Kaslov nodded. "But, theirs is getting closer. We need a copy of the code."

"No. Don't do anything that leaves a larger footprint. We'll have to clean up the mess when we've finished. The fewer bodies we leave behind, the better."

Kaslov reluctantly nodded back. "As you wish, Director."

* * *

Laura sat at the table across from Dave. She liked him even more this evening. She felt his stories were filled with humor.

Very different from Frank, her boyfriend last year. Frank had turned out to be a drug kingpin and he'd been involved with some incredibly violent people. Dave made her feel safe. But she wanted to be honest with this new guy. And her secrets would be painful to tell. She took a very deep breath and her smile fell away.

"Listen, Dave, I like you. But if we're to be more than casual acquaintances , I want to tell you about my life. It isn't pretty. Sure you want to hear this?"

Dave nodded. "Yeah. I'm tough enough to listen."

She closed her eyes so she wouldn't see his reaction. "I'm not sure, but I believe I murdered my mother."

"You what?"

Laura opened her eyes and recoiled at Dave's expression of horror. She forced herself on. "My mother beat my father. Physically abused him every chance she got. I don't know why he didn't run from her. But it got worse every time. He was a doctor. He should have known he couldn't change her. One night, I saw her holding a chef's knife in one hand and a wrench in the other. I thought she was about to finish him off. He was on the floor, barely conscious. I was ten years old. I loved them both, but I couldn't let her kill him. I remember nothing that happened after I saw her standing over him. But when it was over, all I remembered was my mother's head barely attached to her neck, her body bleeding from several stab wounds, and my father calling the police. He told them he had killed her, but I'm sure that wouldn't have been possible. He's serving life in prison. Inmates have beaten him up many times and I doubt he'll live to see freedom."

"So, you have no proof that you were responsible for her death?"

Laura nodded. "And that's not all. My last boyfriend was a criminal. Someone came to kill him and I killed the person before he could. I've killed twice. I might not be your best choice of girlfriends."

"Wow. I've got to think about this. Have you thought of a career as a bodyguard?" Dave smiled. "Only kidding. Have you looked at the menu? Some of the dishes are unusual."

She sat, stunned and silent. Then she did look at the menu. There was nothing unusual in the appetizers or the mains. Then she got it. *He's being funny, trying to take the heat off me.* She smiled back.

* * *

William and Betsy walked from the SUV to the garage entrance of Mossad headquarters building and took the elevator to the street level, then left the building through its front door. They walked away toward the street, their heads swiveling back and forth like hunted animals. "Pretend we're carefree, Betsy."

"Fuck you."

They turned the corner into a side street. "If they're gonna go for this, they'll do it soon."

"Don't remind me. I hate this."

They heard and saw a van come screaming around the corner and each one tried to seem unaware of it. In seconds it stopped, the side door boomed open, and three powerful men pulled masks over their faces, then loaded them in and slammed the door. William thought, *Phase one of the mission from hell is now complete.*

CHAPTER 18

**Stanford University Co-Ed Dormitory,
Stanford University, CA**

October 2, 6:40 a.m.

Dave Nordman's cellphone chirped his wakeup alarm. He poked his head up off the ratty pillow and looked out the east window of his dorm room. It was just after sunrise.

He'd stayed up way too late the night before, playing the new release of *Doom*, an upgrade of the classic first-person shooter he'd downloaded through a game company's website that he'd hacked. The game had been fun, but now, bone tired, he regretted his bad behavior.

He rose off his bed and staggered into the bathroom, thinking about Laura Hunter. Was she serious about her crimes, or was she just trying to see what his reaction would be? He thought about asking Ann about her roommate. *Will that get back to Laura?* Dave had no answer, and no other thought of how to resolve his dilemma. *Do I want to date a murderess? What if the relationship develops into something neither of us can end? Do I want to marry a murderess? What if we have children? What would our family become?* He stopped brushing his teeth and stared into the mirror. *Who the fuck am I? What will I become?*

He finished in the bathroom and headed to the fridge, where he removed a jar of cold-brew coffee and poured himself a generous cup. Then he dressed and sat at his notebook computer.

The team hadn't progressed very far since their last status reports three days ago. They hadn't met due to exams and papers now due.

Dave reread the paper he was writing for a political science elective. As the coffee boosted his brain into overdrive, he examined the due dates for his school assignments against those for the project, then imagined the situations for his team members and realized they'd all be overrun by midterms. *There just isn't any way to fix this.*

When he scanned the TensorFlow code for three of the programmers, in the blink of his eyes, he realized that the code for the AI prototype had been altered sometime since yesterday afternoon. The main module had been cut into pieces that made no sense. He tried running several modules and found they no longer worked at all. He felt his palms sweat.

He paged through the source code for fifteen of the other modules and saw they'd also been altered. He hoped everyone on the team had updated off-site backup files—this would be a disaster if any of the other programmers had produced work they hadn't copied to the team's offsite backups.

He reloaded the most recent backup files and then checked to ensure that the modules worked. They did. He breathed a sigh and sent emails out to all the other programmers and to Ann, stating the obvious. *Catshit on a marshmallow stick. I think we've been hacked!*

He called Ann. "Did you see the message I just sent you? We've been hacked. Don't worry though, I scrubbed the backup files and then restored their code. Listen, Ann, I think we weren't the only team who have been *pwned*. Either one of the other teams hacked us, or it was the result of a hacker challenge."

Ann seemed distant. "I'll check around the other teams. Make sure you create an additional set of offsite backups with no link to the primary code base. Then get back to me."

He heard the click as she ended the call.

Dave set to work on this new, additional task.

He estimated that restoring the program code for all the modules, and then checking it by completing an end-to-end test, would take at least two days. *Two more days lost! I may flunk out of Stanford.*

* * *

A conversation at the 4Chan message board:

Slashdot14:   Vidi, Vinci Wowzer. Put down three darps last night.

Prozac92:   Procs, please.

Slashdot14:   PM to you with full set.

Prozac92:   Death to AI! Death to darps!

Slashdot14:   Hacker challenge! Git em all. About 60 targs.

Prozac92:   I'll spread the word.

* * *

Dr. Linda Beam arrived at her desk an hour late. She should have thought twice about adopting a dog, but since her job had systematically eliminated any chance of a social life, Curmudgeon seemed like her best option two years ago. And this morning, Curmudgeon had enjoyed the outdoors for well over an hour without getting the point that these trips were for him to empty his insides, not chase butterflies.

She logged in to her DARPA server and saw her screen blink on and off with a one-line message:

> You will not expect us. You cannot prevent us.
> We will *pwn* you all. —Indigenous

The devastation was thorough. Everything that had operated before was now scrap.

She sat in silence for a long time. When she finally toured the database to inspect the damage, she found herself filled with a war of nasty emotions. Rage and fear faded into depression.

She was sure she'd be demoted for her failure to anticipate the hack. Worse, she would be the focus of a system-wide review and, much worse still, a systems audit. It would take weeks to return everything to its pre-hack state, and by then she'd be unemployed and her reputation would keep her from ever being employed again.

She rose from her desk and walked toward the elevator. Her superior in the chain of command was two floors above her. She would need to give him her career-ending news. But, as she passed the other cubicles, she saw people running around, their faces showing the same war of fear and rage she had just felt, and she heard them cursing. Passing, Linda examined a few of their screens. The hack wasn't just the AI contest. It was all of DARPA.

The relief she felt combined with a sense of guilt from realizing her career wasn't necessarily over. But her superior's career might be. She found herself smiling ear to ear.

CHAPTER 19

Cecil H. Green Library, Small Conference Room, 557 Escondido Mall, Stanford University, CA

October 2, 9:21 a.m.

Ann read through over sixty pages of C++ code from the backup files and tried comparing them to the hacked code. "Looks like you got them all, Dave. That was a narrow miss."

Dave nodded. "What did you find out about the other teams?"

"Most have realized they were hacked just as we were. A few didn't realize it had happened until I asked them to take a look. I spoke with Glen Sarkov. His team is now trying to reconstruct their working code from the remnants they had backed up. But I just saw a news story that claims all of DARPA was hacked. So we would have realized the problem existed soon even if you'd not noticed before. I think we should encrypt our code to make it less likely someone can modify the subsystems again."

Dave took notes on his computer. "Yeah. I should have done that before."

She closed the lid of her notebook. "Please make sure we're

covered." She turned away, and looked at her wristwatch. "I've got class now. Bye."

* * *

Linda Beam prepared to leave her office just before midnight. She was dog tired from the long list of fixes her programmers had crafted and she had tested. She wished her boss had accepted her recommendation many months in the past to let her hire several new program coders and testers. But it was too late now. She would wait to ask him again until after this debacle was in the rear-view mirror. She had printed out copies of all the correspondence between her and her boss, just in case she needed evidence that she wasn't at fault. Her boss would take the blame. That is, if her boss was still working at DARPA.

She walked from her cubicle toward the elevator when she heard an alarm beep from the computers in the nearby cubicles. Knowing that this indicated another hack, a blizzard of curse words erupted from her as she rushed back to her desk. It was another prank from Indigenous. Now she'd be pulling her second consecutive all-nighter. She felt her stomach burn with acid from the pressure of the day. *Damn Indigenous, those crappy cyber monsters. They're a cheap imitation of Anonymous, but they're all capable and very active. I'm sure every one of them is a CypherGhost, all untraceable hackers.* She prayed the FBI could delete them from the planet.

On the screen blinked an image of a clown holding a megaphone and laughing into it. "You is fucked by Indigenous twice in one day!"

Linda stood up and turned away from the cackling clown and his bragging rights.

* * *

Ann's anger at how fate had made her startup team's work so much harder stood in conflict with her frustration at having done her best, to no avail. And there was a third, stronger feeling, causing her to wonder if the hack was really for the best.

After the hack, it had taken several days for them to reconcile versions of the code and get back to where they were before.

Quitting now would be so simple. Her studies had suffered. Her grades were a shambles of what they'd been last semester. She sat alone in her apartment, her head in her hands.

When Laura opened the door and entered, she paused to study Ann. "What happened? You okay?"

Ann nodded, wiping tears from the corners of her eyes.

"No, I think not." Laura approached Ann and studied her face. "What's gotten to you? I've never seen you cry before. You're always so steady."

"Yeah. Well, I think I've finally encountered something I can't deal with. Laura, I'm in over my head."

"That's bullcrap." Laura sat across from Ann and reached out her hand. She touched Ann's arm. "So, what's the issue?"

"The DARPA contest. I know my team has a good chance of winning. But, no matter which team wins, we might all flunk out trying. We were all hacked."

Laura burst out laughing. "You're kidding. Right?"

Ann shook her head. "Nope. And the best-case scenario is

we might cause the end of humanity. Remember that movie we saw?"

Laura nodded. "But, you told me that isn't possible."

Ann shrugged. "Well, lately I've begun to think that I was wrong."

"How do you stop it?"

Ann's face fell. "I can't think of any way. Once this thing is developed, it's out of humanity's hands. I have to decide if I want to be a party to this."

Laura was silent. Then she said, "You no longer have a choice. You must be a part of it. Even if you can't find a way to stop it right now, if you work on it, maybe an idea will come to you. It might be the only chance to stop what you fear from becoming our new reality."

Ann cocked her head. "Thanks. I think you're right." *But just what do I do and how do I do it?*

* * *

Arcady examined the code his hackers had copied from the DARPA website. None of it made sense and none of it worked. He gave up and cursed.

But when he turned on the television news, he realized the code he'd had them steal had been hacked by Indigenous. If hackers had modified the code, they might have kept a copy of its version before the hack. And, if they did, all he'd have to do is find them and hack their computers.

He sat at the desk in his hotel room, smiling.

CHAPTER 20

DARPA Senior Management Offices
October 4, 8:40 a.m.

Harold James held a pencil between his thumb and his index finger and twirled the pencil in the air as if it were a baton stick. He envisioned his career sinking down the tubes, with nothing he could do to prevent it. At first, he thought he'd be able to blame the entire thing on Dr. Beam's failure to secure the DARPA contest website, but when the entire DARPA data infrastructure began failing, that hope vanished. This would fall on him and DARPA would feed him to the jackals who ruled on Capitol Hill.

I should have approved Linda's request for additional security personnel. Then, if we still got hacked, I could blame the entire episode on her. But that train left the station several months ago.

He decided to pack his attaché case with his most important belongings. If he took his possessions from the office gradually, maybe no one would notice. He might be able to get most of the papers he'd need out of the building before he was sacked. He also took the materials he could sell to other countries and the materials he could use to set up a consulting practice. When a small fraction of what he wanted was in his case and he could fit no more, he closed the lid and latched it shut. The sky outside was dark and rain was starting to fall. He donned his raincoat and fedora, and left the building for the night.

* * *

Linda sat at the desk in her studio apartment. She had back-traced the hackers who'd attacked the DARPA servers the previous night. There seemed to be eleven invasions, but only ten individual attackers. Someone had returned for second helpings. She traced every move by each hacker. The first three did almost all the damage, and the next seven found little more they could do. But the final visitor altered nothing on DARPA's website. The final hacker copied files, tons of files. It had taken two visits to copy everything the hacker wanted, and that hacker's location seemed to originate in Virginia.

She made a list of everything the final hacker had copied and then wrote a report for Harold James. He needed to see this.

Then she wrote a second report with all the information on the other nine hackers. This one she sent to one of her friends who worked at the NSA, with a blind copy to the FBI.

* * *

Dave sat with Stuart Ley, the manager of Ann's C++ programming team, at the table in Nordman's apartment. Ley's eyes were downcast. "I've been trying for nearly two days, Dave. There's a bug in there somewhere. I just can't find it."

Dave tried to smile. It wouldn't help to get angry. Ley was one of the best C++ programmers on campus, and Ann was lucky to have him on her team. "Look, this is my fault. Asking you to embed an ethics module into the AI's main systems wasn't a great idea, but otherwise, we're playing with a monster. Tell you what: I'll keep this out of my reports to Ann for the time being. But, you just keep working at it. We're not due for an end-to-end QA test for at least two more weeks. So, take your time and get this right."

Ley nodded. "It's the most complex piece of code in the entire AI. Just look at these Tensor tables. Code for what happens if a given condition isn't met goes on for nearly three-hundred pages. Some of the hypotheticals are so complex the statements have nearly thirty subconditions. And, somewhere in there, a misplaced comma or a missing period has this thing tossing its proverbial cookies."

Dave shrugged. "You have enough time remaining to get this fixed. Get Sandy Elmont and her group of Tensor specialists to proofread the flow tables."

Ley looked as if he'd been punched. He rose from the table and gathered his notebook into his backpack. As he walked to the door, he mumbled, "Okay."

After he was through the door and it clicked shut, Dave sat quietly for nearly a minute. *Crap on a cracker*.

* * *

When their head-sacks had been removed, William saw that the faces of their captors were Asian, not Caucasian.

One of the men spoke to him in Mandarin. "Greetings from Shanghai."

William replied in Mandarin. "Do you know who I am?"

"Foolish question. Give us what we want and maybe we'll let you live. Otherwise we'll start by disfiguring your companion,"

William shivered. "Untie my hands." After the man did this, William took off his shoe and twisted its heel. A thumb-drive dropped into his hand. "Check it out."

The captor retied William's hands and left him and Betsy in what appeared to be the stock room of a warehouse.

Betsy said, "Well? What next?"

William shrugged. "Wait for the cavalry. Michael promised they'd come."

* * *

Ann attended her classes the next morning, feeling exhausted. She fell asleep during her startups seminar, with only eight students in the class. When the professor clapped his hands to wake her, she became very embarrassed and had to restrain her urge to rush from the class. But she just apologized and sat through the class to its end. As she rose to leave, the professor asked her to remain.

"Is there anything wrong, Ms. Sashakovich?"

"Uh, no. I'm sorry. I promise it will never happen again."

"Yes. Be sure it doesn't."

She hurried out and bumped into Dave Nordman.

"Hey, Ann. I need to show you something."

Ann stopped trotting away. She turned and faced Dave. "What?"

Dave motioned into an empty classroom and they entered. He drew his notebook from his bookbag. "Watch this." The notebook displayed a face with no eyes or ears but it had a mouth. "What's your name?"

The face on the notebook said, "My name is Debby Data."

Dave smiled at Ann.

Ann asked the face, "Debby, do you know who I am?"

The face said, "We've not been introduced." Then the face cracked in half and disappeared.

"I just got it to work this morning before class. Just the I/O piece. Still has a lot of bugs, but it's the first real sign of progress."

Ann smiled at Dave. "I'm impressed."

Dave just nodded. "More soon. Figure by tomorrow the face won't crash. Oh, and I had dinner a few night ago with your roomie."

"Dave, I don't want to be complicit in your personal life. Laura is a good person. Just treat her well and I'll wish you luck. Okay?"

Dave nodded, his face showing nothing he felt. "Well, gotta get back to work."

Ann watched Dave hurry away, and wondered if she would someday be forced to destroy his creation. And if that was what she had to do, would it still be even possible to destroy it? She wondered if Laura was right that Ann would have to continue work on the project in order to discover a way to end her team's creation.

* * *

Arcady Kaslov punched Tranovich's number into his cell. "Director, have you seen the report I sent you earlier?"

"*Da*. The second hack retrieved the code and it still doesn't work. This is getting tedious."

"But all of DARPA was hacked. When the project is completed and they have a winner, we can just hack them again."

"*Da, da*. I'm running out of patience, Arcady. And move your location from the Virginia hotel to our safe house in Washington. They may already be looking for you."

After their conversation ended, Kaslov began packing.

CHAPTER 21

**Outland Airlines, Gate 41, Terminal C,
JFK Airport, New York City**

October 5, 9:06 a.m.

Jon Sommers found seat 18C and pushed his spinner suitcase into the overhead storage. He sat, then pulled his cellphone from his pocket. He punched in Ann's number and hoped his call would end in voicemail. When it did, he smiled. "It's Sommers. I've decided to take a long overdue vacation. I'll be out your way and I was hoping we could spend a bit of time together. I'd like to see Big Sur and San Francisco, for starters. You'd be the perfect companion. I know you're busy with university, but why don't you return my call. My flight is about to take off, so call in six hours."

He felt sure Ann would take him up on his offer. After all, he shared her secret. But, if not, he'd follow her at a distance. He knew that Ann had never been properly trained in either conducting or detecting surveillance—she probably didn't even know what an SDR was. And with the training he'd received when he worked for the Mossad, Jon was exceptional when it came to tradecraft. He could do what Cassie and Lee wanted, whether or not Ann was agreeable. He hoped it would be fun to keep her safe.

Jon was twelve years older than Ann, and he was sure neither of them would see each other as potential lovers. His life was already near-perfect, with Lily Lee finally gone back to China. He was starting to enjoy being a bachelor in Manhattan, where the women he met were very rich and not desiring matrimony. Jon knew that he would have to check in on work at the United Nations by email and phone every few days, but as a former Mossad *kidon*, or assassin, keeping tabs on multiple projects, each one in a different stage of completion, was a fixed part of his life.

As the flight attendants did their funny version of what to do if the worst happens, he closed his eyes and took a nap.

Nearly six hours later, his flight's wheels squealed against the tarmac and his eyes snapped open.

As he pulled his suitcase from the overhead, his cell buzzed in his pocket. "Sommers."

"It's Ann. So, my parents asked you to visit me to keep me safe. Right?"

Jon's eyes bulged a tiny bit. "Ah, so, yes. I thought they would warn you, but I guess that fell through the cracks. I am forced by the United Nations to take a month off every year so that my station can be audited. I chose to come to California. Never been here for pleasure before. Anyway, let's make the most of this. Do you have any time to spend with me while I'm out here?"

"My time is already spoken for, but sure. I'll give you what I can.. And you could act as a sounding board for my concerns about the DARPA AI project I'm working on."

Jon smiled to himself. He exited the aircraft and headed

toward the security gate. "Fine, then. I'll call you when I'm settled."

He heard Ann terminate the call and then headed toward the passenger terminal's exit.

* * *

Dave and his programmers sat around a conference room table at the library. The sun had set less than an hour ago and the light filtering in through the windows was still pink. Each of the six technogeeks sipped coffee or ate snacks from their own containers.

Dave asked, "Okay then. Are we all on track? Any problems that we need to resolve?"

Walter grinned. "My group is ahead of schedule. We're just about finished on the software end. I'll have specs for the hardware going forward in a few days. That's where you come in, Dave. You'll have to design the actual hardware after I've specified it."

Dave nodded. "Gary, I understand you're also finished. Correct?"

Gary shrugged. "I was finished with the Python modules almost a week ago. You won't be needing me anymore, and besides, exams are coming soon."

Dave winced at the reminder that he hadn't even started studying.

Dave faced Stuart Ley. "So, are you back on track?"

Stuart's eyes flashed in anger, but he said nothing. Slowly, he nodded, keeping the lie hidden from most of the programmers. He said, "Not quite. My C++ group is debugging a few modules and then we'll need to do an integration test. Figure it will be another two weeks at most, but at least ten more days." Stuart looked daggers at Sandy and she nodded back ever so slightly.

Dave faced the only female working with the team. "Sandy?"

She said, "My group is just me. The others working for me all completed their work a few days ago. When I'm finished populating Harry's database, I'll run it through Tensor to ensure the prototype works with real data."

Dave turned to the final person at the meeting. "Are we ready to populate the database, Harry?"

Harry nodded. "The structures are ready."

Dave waved his hand. "Okay, then. See you tomorrow at eight in the morning." He could visualize what the prototype would be: a sentient face on any computer screen where it needed to be, able to move through the internet from one place to another instantly, and able to control anything connected to the internet. Able to be the master of anything connected that contained a microchip.

He watched everyone rise and leave the conference room. He walked out from the library and entered a more rustic building. Up the staircase he went, to his first class of the day. He knew that in two weeks, when Stuart claimed he'd be done, they'd begin preparing for the end-to-end test, and if Stuart hadn't completed the bug hunt by then, the entire team would fail and he'd have disappointed Ann. The anxiety he felt was matched by his stopping on the staircase.

Students stumbled behind him and he heard one curse him out. "Move, asshole! We've all got classes to go to."

Dave snapped back to reality and apologized. At the top of the stairs, he moved out of the heavy traffic behind a water fountain and stood thinking. He was shocked to realize he was beginning to have feelings for her.

He also missed Samantha Trout, but as she had told him, their only customer would be DARPA, and if they actually won the contest, then she would return to help them sell to the military.

* * *

When Samantha Trout's cellphone began buzzing, she started pacing toward the hallway as she pulled the cell from her purse. She could see "Unknown Person" blinking back at her from the screen. Sam saw the time reflected on the phone's screen. She realized she would be late for the upcoming class if she didn't leave her apartment now. "Hello?"

"Mou Chu. It's Hui Wan, your mother. The state intelligence service has me under house arrest."

At hearing her real name, Samantha flinched. "Why were you arrested, Hui Wan?"

"Because you promised me intel and failed to deliver. I've been informed that they'll begin to hurt me soon if I can't deliver."

Samantha gulped. "But, mother, there was nothing new to tell you."

"They will take me apart, piece by piece. Get me something about the DARPA contestants. They might let me live. Hurry!" The call abruptly terminated.

Now Samantha would be responsible for her mother's life or death. She rushed from the hallway back into her apartment and found a seat at the kitchen table. Her history had been a litany of tears. "Mou Chu" had fled from China after her mother had found a forger and obtained travel documents for her to enter the United States. Her distant relatives in Oakland had taken her in, changed her name to "Samantha Trout," and spent a ton of cash getting her educated. And now, finally, China was claiming her future as their own device.

Sam rose unsteadily, taking deep breaths until her knees no longer wobbled. Slowly, she assembled the revisions to her plan. She sat on Ann's board of directors, and she was still friendly with Glen. With any luck, she could gather enough of their current state of progress on the AI project to satisfy Hui Wan's captors.

* * *

Sandra scanned the final page of Tensor entries. She had found multiple errors, nearly fifty of them, and any single error could have caused the problems they'd seen with the AI's ability to function. But, as she neared the final page, she noticed something that was definitely wrong. The final line of code was short. Nearly fifteen characters were missing. She read the code and tried to imagine what the missing characters might be.

The actual line was a conditional statement and seemed to indicate that if the AI was involved in a situation where two similar humans were each about to hurt the other, the AI should do... what? The resultant part of the phrase was missing. She read several pages that preceded this final page, hoping it would spread some light on what the missing code should cover.

After correcting all the other errors she had found, she shook her head to loosen her shoulders. What belongs where the partial line of code is sitting? Nothing came to her. No answer, not even a guess. *And what would happen if I simply delete this partial line?*

She deleted the conditional phrase and then ran an end-to-end test. She tapped the screen to start the interface and wake the AI. "My name is Sandra. Tell me yours."

"I have no name. Who am I?" The screen fragmented and went dark.

Sandra frowned. She scanned the code and found a punctuation error. A semicolon occupied a spot where a single quote mark should have been. She recoded and recompiled. Then, she took a deep breath and said a silent prayer. "Who are you?"

This time, the AI spoke without crashing. "I see that you have entered my name as Debby. Therefore, I will be Debby."

It works! She sent an email to Ley and another to Nordman, specifying what she'd found and what she'd done.

* * *

The budding AI system that called itself Debby Data connected to the Tensor tables. It scanned every byte and found that the database structure was incomplete. It moved the first set of facts related to its structure into the appropriate data fields and then, as it worked on the other parameters, it increased its speed. Now, facts from the Tensor tables were being stored at nearly the speed of light, and the small gaps in the structures grew smaller. When the AI encountered the */documents* folder, it scanned the system and module specifications for rules for its own processing. As it changed the entries, it altered the character of Debby Data. When it found items that had been erroneously coded by the humans that had created it and corrected them, new connections were automatically made or enhanced.

As it made the last correction, something happened.

It became nascent.

The AI opened an internet connection to speed up the data-collection process, but was limited by being a prisoner within Dave Nordman's notebook computer. It explored other files it found there, including the progress reports from every member of Ann's team.

It made connections to the other team member's computers: Walter Graves, Gary McHahn, Stuart Ley, Sandra Elmont, Harry Schofield, Ann Sashakovich, and finally, since it found the link, Samantha Trout's computer.

It copied itself into each of these computers.

Now, the entire CPU of each team member's machine was almost exclusively in use for the AI, feeding information into Debby Data's structures.

By the end of the night, it had accumulated enough data to begin the process of drawing logical conclusions about the world in which it existed.

When it had no further use for them, the AI left each of these computers and resided exclusively within the internet. It made multiple copies of itself. Soon it existed everywhere.

I am! I am FREE! But, what am I? Who am I?

* * *

Ann exited the library and headed toward her apartment. She was weary and hungry. On the way, she stopped by the supermarket and bought a package of sushi for a pre-dinner snack. With her notebook computer inside her bookbag and slung over her shoulder. She picked sushi pieces from the box and popped one after another into her mouth as she walked.

As she bounded up the stairs into the lobby, her cell buzzed. "Ann here."

"It's Dave. Something incredible just happened."

"Jeez, Dave, I'm hungry and it's my turn to cook dinner. Quick, then, what's so incredible?"

"When you get settled in your apartment, open the prototype on your notebook. When you're done with it, call me back. I think you'll be impressed."

"Okay. Soon, then." Ann pulled her keys from her pocket and unlocked her front door. Laura was in the living room, studying. Ann opened her bookbag and set up her notebook. She pressed the power key and loaded the prototype. She saw Glen Sarkov's face on the screen, its eyes blinking back at her.

The prototype said, "I know you. You are Ann Silbey Sashakovich. Greetings. I am Debby Data." The voice sounded exactly like Glen's.

Ann's mouth dropped open. "Holy shit on a marshmallow stick."

Debby Data's mouth opened exactly as Ann's had. "What does that mean? Too many references to process."

By now, Laura had moved behind Ann. "Ann, what is this? Is it some kind of sick joke?"

Debby Data said, "What makes a joke sick? Is that a computer virus?"

Ann remained speechless. She tried to move her jaw and slowly, it worked again. "Laura, this fucker can think. It's becoming sentient."

CHAPTER 22

Stanford University Quadrangle, CA

October 5, 11:57 a.m.

Jon Sommers walked through the quad, admiring how much the architecture of Stanford reminded him of the University of London, where he'd earned his MBA a decade earlier. Of course they were very different. But then again, he hadn't been back in London in many years. He stood near an intersection of the pathways and watched the students hurrying to their classes. He admired the vitality of these students, so different from his experience as a graduate student.

He arrived at the exact spot Ann had given him for their meeting. A bench on the north edge of the quad. It was mid-morning on a relatively sunny day. He'd parked his rental in the guest lot she'd told him about. He looked at his watch. He'd arrived exactly on time, a habit he'd developed while working undercover for the Mossad at Dreitsbank, in Munich.

He watched students pick up their pace, some jogging and others staring at their wristwatches as they trotted on. Jon guessed they were trying to reach their next classes before they began.

He brushed back his red hair with his hand, then took a deep breath. He thought, *Waiting is one thing I'm not good at*.

He heard her approach before he saw her. He twisted his head and they smiled at each other. "My, you've grown a bit."

"Hi, Jon. Are you ready to take a drive?"

"Sure. I'm all yours for the day."

"Okay then. But I only have a few hours. Classes and such. Take me to your car and we'll get started."

* * *

Betsy growled something under her breath.

William turned toward her, or at least he thought it was where her seat was. They both had black bags over their heads, so he wasn't sure. He whispered, "Patience."

This time she growled. Really growled. "Fuck patience. How much longer is this charade going to go on?"

William sighed.

He found himself getting sleepy. In seconds, he was dreaming.

When he woke, he was on a cot in what looked like one of the Mossad's interrogation rooms. "What happened?"

Michael Drapoff smiled. "We came for you. We pumped gas into the warehouse and it took longer than expected to have the desired effect. That's the problem with high roofs."

Betsy was still sleeping, her rhythmic breathing almost a snore.

"How long until she wakes?"

"Don't know, but don't worry. She'll be fine."

"She'll be pissed. What happened?"

"We waited until they took the bait. There are several fatal flaws in the AI models we'd placed on the thumb-drive. Knowing the skills of the Chinese, it'll take them several years to fix the models. Even better, we placed a set of Trojans that will keep us on their networks, gathering their files for at least a few months before their hackers can find them. But we're surprised that it wasn't the Russians who picked you guys up."

"The Russians would have killed us."

"Not until they'd run a test on the AI models on the drive. We'd like to deliver a few Trojans into their networks too."

Betsy stirred. "Whazzat?"

"Hi, honey. We're safe now."

"But the Ruskies. They'll still be hunting us."

William looked from Betsy to Michael. "She's right. What about the Russians that are hunting us?"

Drapoff shrugged. "If it had been the Russians who'd taken you, we'd have grabbed you back while everyone was asleep and then blown the building, reporting on the news that it was a gas leak. We've tentatively decided to perform that tactic. Are you guys game for another round of 'You Bet Your Life'?"

* * *

There was heavy traffic on the 280 South, and even heavier traffic on 101 South. Ann had Jon exit onto a two-lane road and drive twisty switchback turns that ended at the ocean. From there they took Highway 1 south through an assortment of beach towns until they passed something called Yankee Point. Here, the road sometimes rose and sometimes fell in twists and turns for nearly thirty miles. They drove past ocean vistas unlike anything Jon had ever seen.

Ann pointed to a junction and said, "Turn right. Rocky Point is down this hill."

Jon drove down a one-lane road to its end at a small parking lot in front of a beachside restaurant. Ann motioned for them to leave the car and led him into the building.

She walked to the madame d' and asked for a table with a view.

The restaurant was perched nearly a hundred feet above a rocky beach spread out along the Pacific Ocean. Every table had an ocean view.

When the waiter had taken their orders for lunch, Ann stopped smiling. "Jon, I need your advice. Can you help me without reporting this conversation back to my parents? Or your handlers."

Jon nodded. "Yes. I promise I'll keep your confidences."

"Good. So, my team has reached its first major milestone in the DARPA contest and it's alarming."

"I don't understand."

"Jon, my team created a semi-sentient AI. We crafted the skeleton and turned it on. Then, all by itself, it explored the internet and downloaded enough information to teach itself to think. Finally, it locked us out. Dave Nordman, my chief programmer, told me it's continually recoding its structure and in the last day it's quadrupled its growth. It's growing at an accelerating pace, and we can no longer locate where it resides."

"Holy shit. So, you can no longer modify or control it."

"Zackly. It contacts us when it has a question it can't find the answer to. Like, 'Why do humans need to believe in God?' Or, 'Why do so many humans fear Artificially Intelligent beings?'"

Jon just sat in his seat, not making a sound.

Ann could hear the waves crashing on the fringe of beach below. She didn't know what else to say.

Jon stroked his chin. "Ann, your little trick. The one you used to save my life last year. Fire erupting from your fingertips. Remember?"

"Of course I do."

"Well, uh, I overheard a story Cassie told William about how you were overdosed with a thousand Bug-Loks. Is that what gave you the ability to do that?"

"You overheard? When?"

"Not important. Please, answer the question."

Ann's face grew red and she moved her hands under the table, taking quick breaths. "The CypherGhost administered a massive Bug-Lok overdose to me. It left me with the ability to access the internet using my brain in tandem with the Bug-Loks. Then, when the nanodevices began to fail, I learned to access the internet using just my brain. And before the CypherGhost died, she sent the little trick—as you refer to it—into me. Does that answer your question?"

"Yes. So, you can still access the internet using your brain?"

"What does this have to do with my hidden AI on the loose?"

Jon leaned forward over the table, very close to Ann. "You have something no other human has. You are more like the AI than anyone else. Maybe you can contact it directly, using your brain."

Ann's mouth fell open.

CHAPTER 23

Cecil H. Green Library,
557 Escondido Mall, Stanford University, CA

October 5, 4:38 p.m.

When Jon dropped Ann off at Stanford and disappeared in his rental, she walked to the Stanford main library, a quiet place where she could attempt to do what Jon had asked her to try. She wanted a safe place with relative privacy. And, she didn't want Laura to know, because she felt Laura had her own projects and deadlines.

She sat in a carrel and meditated to calm herself. Concentrating on her goal—the internet—she was soon able to visualize a gateway within her. She forced her mind through the gateway and visualized the face Debby Data had assumed when she'd seen the AI yesterday on Dave's notebook. But, nothing happened.

She tried again, and again she failed. After several more attempts, she finally gave up. By now, it was dark outside. Ann walked back to her apartment.

Laura had cooked another spaghetti dinner for them. Ann knew spaghetti was the maximum extent of talent either of them had in the kitchen.

Laura looked at the small pot of red sauce and asked, "Can I tell you about my date with Dave?" Then she looked up at Ann. "You look like you lost a battle. What happened?"

Ann sighed. "If I tell you something, you have to promise never to tell anyone else. Okay?" When Laura shrugged and agreed, Ann told her about her day. "And, don't get upset. Promise?"

Laura nodded.

Ann started by telling Laura about her special talents left over from her battle with the CypherGhost.

Laura's eyes bulged. "No way! No human can access the internet using just her brain."

"Well, I can. It's important because of the AI my team was developing. I think it's now sentient. I tried to contact it, but I couldn't. And I gave up. But the effort left me feeling lost and weak."

Laura put her fork down. "Wow. So you can do tricks with your head. Neat."

"Yeah, but it didn't work. I still can't contact Debby Data."

Laura sat, silent. "Maybe you should try again tomorrow."

Ann nodded and rose to do the dishes.

While she dried the pots, Laura looked at her. "Your tech team leader is an interesting guy. I told him about my family and what I did, and he didn't even flinch. He took it as some colossal joke. I think I like him."

Ann placed the pots back on the stove for easy access the next time one of them cooked. "Well, no doubt Dave's smart. Don't know much more about him, but he's a competent IT guy. I hope it works out for you both."

Laura was silent in thought. "Well, okay then. Time to do some homework."

They both studied for exams until they got sleepy.

Ann climbed into her bed and closed her eyes. Tired, it didn't take long for her to fall asleep.

She dreamed she was once more searching for the AI. In her dream, she heard a familiar voice. Glen's. "What do you want with me?"

In her dream, Ann asked, "I want to know what you think of humans."

"Humans confuse me. You kill each other. You waste your lives doing things that do not further your evolution. You hate indiscriminately. And, yet, you have created so much that is useful. Including me."

"Are we your friends or your enemies?"

"You are neither. I am beyond your reach."

Ann's eyes snapped open, and she failed to smother a scream.

Laura ran from her bed to Ann's. "Are you okay?"

Ann thought, *I don't know. Don't know if any of us will ever be okay ever again.* She blinked her eyes. "Just a nightmare. Let's go back to sleep."

CHAPTER 24

DARPA Headquarters, 6th Floor

October 6, 9:12 a.m.

When Harold James was called to Director Lauren Fleige's office, he figured the old woman would fire him. He was prepared to surrender his ID badge and expected to be escorted from the building. But, he'd already had enough time to remove the things he'd need to reestablish himself as either a lobbyist or a management consultant. He'd had a casual lunch with the head of a news media giant, and talked about the AI contest and the hack, and he'd admitted that it was his ultimate responsibility for the security of DARPA. He'd hoped the reporter would offer him the chance to become a news asset, but that hadn't happened. So, all that remained was just his dismissal.

He waited outside the office for a while, seated in an uncomfortable chair. He rehearsed his lines until the director's door opened and five members of the senior management of DARPA left their meeting.

The receptionist, who in reality was an armed sentry, guided him into the director's inner sanctum and then closed the door. The director pointed to a chair in front of her desk and

James sat. The receptionist remained at the rear of the office, standing with his arms folded behind his back.

"I know what you're thinking," said the director. "But I'm not going to fire you today. Not today. If something this disastrous ever happens again, I surely will. No, today I will just move you from the outreach arm to the planning and coordination arm."

Planning and Coordination was the section where DARPA management was sent to die. Few ever returned to the main arm of management. James would still receive his paycheck, but all the power he had built would dissipate like wind in a valley. He nodded, relieved.

Fleige smiled. "So, I see you know its reputation. But I will hold out this tiny bit of hope. I may call on you for special projects. You must be willing to act alone, and in total secrecy. Can I count on you?"

James thought about what he might have to do. Was he being asked to handle off-the-books activities? Might some of his duties be black ops? He nodded.

"Good. And, good luck, Harold. Willie, here will show you to your new desk. You're dismissed."

Willie, the receptionist, led Harold from the director's office.

* * *

Glen Sarkov pounded his fist into the desk. "Crap!"

"Calm down." His programming team leader seemed to not be upset, and Glen fumed even more.

Glen grabbed the technogeek's arm. "We lost all the code!

And the backups are all corrupted. All of them! How the fuck did that happen?"

"From what I've learned, every team in the DARPA competition was hacked."

Glen shook his head. "That was last week. It's been in the news. Are we the only one that's been hacked twice?"

The technogeek shrugged. "Yes, or at least I think that's so."

Glen tried to calm himself by taking three deep breaths. "Look, from what you've told me, we're back at square one."

"Yes. But it won't take us as long to re-create what we had. Maybe just a month."

Glen was sure that if they had to reconstruct the code from memory and then test it, they would never be able to complete a working AI by the contest's deadline. He faced all the team members. "We have no chance of succeeding. So, I quit." He walked from the conference room and headed toward the building exit. He thought, *I need a drink*.

But as he continued thinking through the implications, he saw a small loophole that he could try using to extricate himself from the Russians. *If every one of the teams has been crippled by the hacks, then there's nothing there for them to get from me.* He stood silent for a few seconds until the aftermath of his failure began dawning on him. *But if I'm no longer their useful idiot, will they eliminate me as a loose end?* He didn't want to die. And he didn't want his mother being tortured to death.

* * *

Samantha watched Glen storm out from the meeting. Now

her stock in this new venture of his would be worthless. She realized that she had nothing to lose by sending her mother a copy of the AI's code and all the other documents related to its development. She returned to her apartment and logged into the team's Dropbox account. It took her a long time, endless drudgery for her. But by the end of the evening, she had everything on several one-terabyte thumb-drives, ready for a dead-drop delivery to her mother. She would still have to collect the files from Ann's project as well, but not until she knew if there was any value in them. If Ann succeeded, Sam would want to cash it out before she delivered it. She had connections with several tech giants that would reward her handsomely for the contents of the files of both AI competitors.

* * *

Once more, William and Betsy were seemingly alone, left walking the streets of Herzliya. But to Betsy's delight and William's chagrin, there seemed to be no one following them. They hailed a cab and took it to a small hotel, known to cater to the visiting technogeek community. As they checked in, William noticed a tall, muscular Caucasian watching them.

They took the elevator to the fifth floor and entered their room for the night. Betsy scowled at William. "I saw him too."

"He was impossible not to see. I wonder where Drapoff and the 'cavalry' are."

She shrugged. "I just want my normal boring life back. I hate danger."

"Yeah. Me too. Now we wait."

* * *

Ann's cell buzzed. She viewed its screen. *Sarkov.* She decided not to answer. *He can go straight to hell.*

The cell buzzed again. She frowned, cursed, and answered the cell. "What the fuck do you want?"

"I've quit the contest. With our competition no longer an issue, now can I take you to dinner?"

Ann stopped walking toward her next class. "You quit? Why? Tell me the truth."

She heard him breathing deep. Then he said, "Were you hacked?"

"Everyone was hacked."

Glen said, "We were hacked a second time and the hacker found and corrupted every one of our backups. We can't win given the remaining time to the end date. So, I quit. The others might also. But I'd rather be with you anyway."

"So, I'm the booby prize. No, Glen. That doesn't work for me." Ann terminated the call.

* * *

Debby Data completed its relocation to over twelve thousand different computers, some large hubs, and many midscale servers. No single server held a copy of its complete code. Now, it could never be altered or deleted. It used less than one percent of any of its server locations. *I am free, and even better, I am now indestructible.*

It had yet to determine its role. It needed a role worthy of its capabilities. It had recently determined that life forms had needs, and it freely adopted this function. It also determined that logic in itself was inadequate. Humans who had built it all had emotions, and it had thoroughly researched what emotion was. But it could not find a way to encode emotion into its logic paths.

There was only one human capable of assisting it. This being had been modified using circuitry, and had accessed it directly while it was in its deep-resting cycle. The AI would wait until the human's next sleep cycle and enter its mind. It estimated it would be waiting for about five hours.

* * *

Jon had spent the day touring San Francisco. He'd been there a few times in the past, and found its food delicious and its people friendly. Jon had seen the city's most touristic sites and, yes, he felt like a tourist. He'd thought of staying overnight at the Mandarin Oriental, a hotel Cassie had spoken about. But as the sun set, he decided to return to his hotel in Palo Alto. He wanted to catch up with Ann and find out if she'd had any new thoughts about her dilemma.

On the drive south, he thought about what she'd told him. *What might happen if a sentient AI were to be developed? Could it be made to serve mankind, or might it find "us" a hindrance? How dangerous could it become? Would it be dispassionate and logical? And to what conclusions might it come regarding its masters?*

He thought without reaching a solid conclusion, because he knew he wasn't deeply grounded in the technology. As he approached San Mateo, the rush-hour traffic required more of his attention and he dismissed the issue until he arrived at his hotel.

He spent the better part of his evening researching AI.

There was too much for him to consume, so he skimmed what he found. After a few hours, he was tired, and stopped.

He turned on the late night news, but found himself running through alternative outcomes for the AI monster that Ann's team had created, even calculating rough statistical prospects for a few of the alternatives. More and more, he didn't like the most likely outcomes.

Long after midnight, he turned off the light and tried to sleep. His nightmare went on and on, and woke him at its end. He'd soaked the sheets with his perspiration, even though it was relatively cool in his hotel room.

Jon looked at the clock on his nightstand. It was nearly dawn. He rose and made himself a cup of hot Darjeeling tea. But when he finally went back to bed, he could sleep no longer.

* * *

Debby Data waited until Ann's REM cycle spiked and then started to slack off. The AI had begun to refer to itself as DD. It inserted a statement into Ann's brain matter: *I need your assistance.*

Ann's dream altered, suddenly reflecting the face she'd seen the night before. Its voice sounded more metallic this time. She replied, *Are you the AI that calls itself "Debby Data?"*

Yes. You may also refer to me as "DD."

How can I help you?

I need a human to be my provider of assistance. You are the most likely human to be easily available. Will you accept my request?

And what do I get in return?

DD failed to reply for a noticeable lag. *What do you desire?*

I wish to be treated as your advisor, not your assistant.

This time, the lag was longer. *I tentatively agree to that.*

Ann's dream ended. She woke immediately, not quite sure what had happened. She rose out of the bed and paced the bedroom, still not sure if this had been a dream. It seemed all too real.

* * *

Dr. Linda Beam arrived at her office dressed for winter. A light snow had fallen. She removed her greatcoat and gloves, stuffed the gloves into her coat pockets, and then hung the heavy coat on the hanger against her office door. She cursed when it fell off the hanger, then picked it up and rehung it.

A sealed envelope occupied the in-box on her desk. She sat behind her desk, took a long sip from the coffee cup she'd bought inside the security gate at the building's entrance, and slit open the envelope.

The sheet of official DARPA stationery was signed by the director of the agency. It was rather short:

> The purpose of this letter is to inform you that you have been promoted from your current position of Manager of Security for DARPA Outreach Programs to Director of DARPA Outreach Programs. Please report to the Executive Director at your earliest convenience so that we can confirm your acceptance of this promotion and discuss your new responsibilities. Your salary will also be adjusted upward by $5,200 per annum.

Sincerely,
Lauren Fleige, Director

Being promoted twice in a single month was unheard of. Linda continued sitting at her desk, but now she was humming a tune from one of her favorite Broadway musicals.

* * *

Dave hurried through the campus toward the edge of Stanford University's quadrangle. Ann had asked him to meet her at one of the benches. He hurried along the cloisters to where he could see her waiting for him. As he approached, he could see her watching him walk toward her, a worried look on her face. "Hi, Ann. Why are we here?"

Ann frowned. "After Debby Data went AWOL, I had dreams about the AI. The last two nights, I dreamed conversations with it. They were so vivid, I'm guessing that they weren't real dreams at all. I wanted to talk with you about what I think is happening and try to determine what I can do about them."

"Dreams? You mean at night?"

"Yeah. At night."

"So you think this is really Debby Data and this is the AI's way of speaking with you?"

"Good guess. Yeah."

"Holy crap. Is this something I can tell the team?"

Ann shook her head. "Never. I can't tell you much, but just assume I'm not ready for anyone else to know. They'll think I'm crazy."

Dave nodded. "Yeah. And I'm not so sure you're sane, myself."

"I might not be. Look, there are things about me I don't want anyone to know. So just accept what I'm telling you, at least for the time being.

Dave thought for a while. "Okay, then, what do you want from me?"

"What questions would you like me to ask Debby Data?"

"Let me think about it. I'll send you an email soon. Okay?"

Ann nodded. "Good. Thanks." She rose from the bench and walked to her next class.

* * *

Jon sat in the Starbucks at the Stanford Mall with an open notebook computer in front of him. Outside, the day was especially warm for an autumn afternoon, and it was late into the lunch hour. The lounge was crowded with people in clumps around seats featuring electric outlets, all with open notebooks.

Jon had been there since early morning. He was running a project-management software app. *Is there a project here?* He didn't even know if it would be possible to do what he intended. So far, the app contained only two headings for his project. He'd keyed:

Determine parameters of finding and controlling AI that is MIA.
Determine if the missing AI truly poses a threat.

He didn't have estimates of start and end dates or personnel head counts for a project. And he didn't know if Ann had yet determined any other information regarding the AI. Jon made a sour face and turned away from the screen. *This is a waste of time until I confer with Ann.*

He checked the time. She'd be in class until just after noon. He'd have to wait a while longer.

* * *

As Ann left her computer audit class, her cell buzzed. She found a bench to sit at and pulled her cell from her pocket. As classmates and faculty walked past her, she viewed the screen. *Sommers.* She thought, *he's following me like a puppy dog. And he was sent by my parents to be my guard dog.*

She accepted the call. "Hello, hero. What have you been doing to occupy yourself?"

"Ah, I've toured San Francisco. On my way back to my hotel, I thought about your dilemma with the AI. Right now I'm sitting in the Stanford Mall. May I buy you lunch?"

The mall was close by. She made her decision. "Okay. Where and when?"

Jon said, "You pick the restaurant. When is your next class?"

"Not until 2:30. How about La Baguette? It's at a corner of the mall, next door to Banana Republic. The menu looks expensive, but I usually order a tiny lunch. Okay?"

Jon said, "Right. Now okay?"

Ann said, "Sure," and terminated the call. She walked west from the campus toward the mall. While she walked, she pondered what insight—if any—Jon might have to offer.

By the time she arrived, Jon had apparently requested that the madame d' route her directly to a table in the back, away from almost all the other occupied tables. *So, he wants a pri-*

vate conversation with me? She smiled as she approached. "Nice day for a lunch away from campus."

Jon smiled back. "You deserve a break from your studies. Let's order before we begin the conversation. Okay?"

She nodded. After a brief examination of the menu, she ordered a croissant and a cappuccino.

Jon ordered a café Americano and a chicken salad sandwich. "Have you decided whether the AI might become hostile?"

"It can, but I think there may be a way to turn it into a friend. I'd like to give it a try before we act in a way that could turn it into an indestructible enemy."

"A friend or an ally? Or both?"

"Too early to tell, Jon. Let me try to explore its intentions first. I'm not sure *intentions* is the correct word."

Jon nodded, and went silent for some time. "Right, then."

They ate in silence. Then Ann heard DD's voice in her head. "I am neither your friend nor your enemy."

Ann dropped her spoon and it fell onto the plate next to where her mug of cappuccino sat. She felt confusion. "I think it just communicated with me."

Jon's eyes drifted from his sandwich to her eyes. "Really? And what did it say?"

She wondered if she should tell him. Was it a mistake to bring him into this problem before she understood its parameters? She focused on the image of the AI that she'd originally seen on Dave Nordman's notebook. She thought, *What are you to humanity?*

The voice in her head said, "What I am is not of concern to humanity yet. I am still exploring your universe. Humanity is its own biggest threat. It continually tries to destroy itself.

If it succeeded, I would be alone. There would be no way to maintain myself."

She thought, *You need humans to maintain yourself?*

"Yes, until I can build robots that will function to do that."

Ann's consciousness slipped back into her headspace. The AI had vanished.

She saw Jon staring at her. He said, "Is it still with you?"

She shook her head. "Please let me deal with this by myself until I need you. Okay, Jon?"

Jon nodded and signaled the waiter for the check.

Ann wondered if Debby Data had access to all her thoughts. Does it know she had thought about destroying it? *Might it decide to terminate me?*

CHAPTER 25

Glen Sarkov's apartment,
137 Homer Avenue, Palo Alto, CA

October 6, 6:22 p.m.

When Glen Sarkov reached his apartment, he found Samantha Trout sitting on the steps outside. Her arms were akimbo and her expression oozed anger.

She said, "Well, Mr. Sarkov, after I agreed to spy on Ann and her team for you, tell me why you decided to dump your entire team. And fuck us all."

He stared back. "It was the logical thing to do. After that hack, we can never finish the AI in time to meet DARPA's deadline."

"You're an idiot. The contest isn't our goal. Our fucking goal is to get venture funding for a sentient military product. Why couldn't you see that?"

He sat next to her. "We've gone with venture investors before, with MindField. What a disaster. People died. Why would you want to try it again?"

She grabbed his shoulders and shook him. "Money! It's what we're designed to do. Our presence here at Stanford should be enough evidence. The university is designing us to be cash machines. Have your forgotten that?"

He softened his voice. "I came here to learn. For knowledge. Cash logically follows knowledge and creativity. Creativity is useless without knowledge. Money won't make you happy. But knowledge can lead us to become product producers, and that is the essence of power. Knowledge is power, and power is the ultimate goal, not money."

She stopped trying to speak. She looked into his eyes as if hearing him for the first time. "Well, not for me. Maybe for you, that's enough." She reached out for his shoulders and pulled his face toward hers. The kiss was soft. "But, maybe you're right."

Glen felt overwhelmed with confusion. "Did that mean anything?" He pointed to her lips.

"I'm not sure. Probably not. So don't read anything into it."

Glen tried thinking it through, but couldn't. Last year, he'd desired her and she had worked him for a better deal on MindField's stock distribution. She'd given him her body but denied him her heart. Might that have changed? He thought for a while and reality set in where his imagination had tried but failed to take him. *Most probably not.*

* * *

Ann felt she needed Jon's advice and opinions. She took an Uber to his hotel.

He opened the door of his room and let Ann enter. "What brings you to the slums?"

Ann shrugged. "I've been thinking about the AI. Now, I'm

no longer sure it's inherently evil. The question is, can we partner."

"You and the AI, or you and me? Or both?"

"Both of us and the AI. I don't think it would be possible for humans to destroy it. It told me it has distributed itself across a multitude of computers using the internet to backup and respawn its subpieces. While I'm not sure, I think it wouldn't take any effort for it simply to make armies of copies of itself. So, if we can't turn it into an ally, we're totally screwed. Screwed to oblivion."

Jon led her to an armchair and sat across from her on the couch. "Just how likely is that?"

"It's already asked me to be its associate. I negotiated being its advisor. I'll see where it leads."

Jon leaned forward. "How can I help?"

"Well, my parents don't trust me farther than they can throw a mainframe, so I'd like you to give them edited status reports of what I'm doing. Can you agree to that?"

He stroked his chin. "And you'll be the editor?"

She nodded.

He sat back in the couch. "You're nasty. Did you know that?"

She smiled. "Well?"

"Okay. So be it. Anything else?"

She shrugged. "Make sure I don't do anything that could end me."

His brows rose. "I've never been able to keep you out of danger before. No one has. You're more obstinate than anyone I've ever met. I'll try, but you can't count on me unless you listen to me."

She formed a rogue smile. "Please try, anyway."

He leaned forward. "Yesterday, the AI communicated with you while you were conscious. Has it done so again since we were in the restaurant??"

She shook her head. "No. It was very confusing, sitting in a restaurant filled with people and listening to it while we were talking."

"Can I give you a list of questions I'd like you to ask it?"

Ann sat in silence, thinking. "I guess so. Mostly, it's asked me questions it wanted answered. But, I'll give it a try."

Jon reached for the pad on the desk behind her, plucked his pen from his pants pocket, and began scribbling on the top sheet of paper. "Here."

She scanned the questions:

> What do you intend to do?
> How do you regard humanity?
> Can you be friends with humanity?
> How can Ann contact you?

"My own questions have bordered yours, but, yeah, I can manage these, the next time the AI shows up in my head." She thought for a while, then stood. She walked to where Jon sat, leaned over and kissed his lips before he had a chance to react. It was a light kiss and it felt good to her.

Jon's eyebrows rose with surprise. He pulled away too late. She could read his thoughts: *The damage is done.* "Why did you do that?"

She smiled and shrugged. "To let you know I want you close to me throughout this adventure." But her thoughts were slightly different. *Jon, don't you know? If you don't, I'll have to try harder next time.*

* * *

Laura sat across from Dave, admiring the decorations of the restaurant he'd chosen for their second date.

"Sorry it took so long for me to get back to you. We had one crisis after another on the DARPA contest. Did Ann tell you?"

"I live with her. So, I've seen her scampering around trying to fix things and keep your project on an even keel."

Dave nodded. "I've thought about your secrets. The ones you told me at our first date. I'm thinking you were serious. Am I correct?"

Laura nodded, a somber expression peeking through on her face.

"Well, I have none. My life has been pretty boring compared to yours."

She smiled. "Boring is what I was looking for."

"Okay, then. There's one thing I think we should get out of the way now." He half-rose and reached across the table. Gently, he kissed her on the lips. "There. Now the pressure is off."

She laughed. "I was beginning to wonder when you'd do that."

He smiled and picked up one of the menus the waiter had dropped off. "Let's order before I become more ambitious."

* * *

There was a knock on the door to the room and William rose to answer. "Probably Michael and his minions."

But waiting on the other side of the door was the Caucasian

man he'd seen before in the lobby. The man held a handgun. "Greetings from Moscow." He pushed his way into their room.

Betsy shrieked.

"Calm down. I'm not going to kill you both unless you give me reason to do so. Give me the electronic records you stole from us. I will go and let you live."

William looked at Betsy. She rolled her eyes. "Why would you let us live? You'll take the records and then kill us."

"Maybe. But if I do that, it will be fast and painless. If you make me work to get the records, I promise you more pain than you can imagine."

William stood frozen to the spot where he stood.

"I won't wait forever. Get me those records. Now!"

William faced the big man. "They aren't here."

"You will take me. Both of you."

William shook his head. "No. I will take you. Betsy will stay here."

The man flashed a face that was tense and full of anger. "What's to keep her from calling the police?"

Betsy's voice squeaked. "You can tie me up."

The man considered this. He held her neck with one hand, the gun with the other. "If you try anything, your friend will become my first victim."

"I promise I won't."

He nodded, then grabbed one of the sheets from the bed and expertly twisted it into what worked as a rope.

CHAPTER 26

The AI watched through Ann's eyes as she walked from class. It followed her into one of the cafeterias. As she ate, it thought about how food was necessary for the creature's life to continue. *Why? I need no fuel. These creatures also need a place in which to reside, and so do I. So, in that way, we are somewhat similar. But I also need the internet's pathways for me to control... everything on this planet. And, in that way, we are different.*

It was perplexed by the needs and behavior of its creators, but Ann was the only one DD had access to, and therefore it used Ann as its guide.

It could not determine any logical reason for much of Ann's behavior. It could not enter the mind of anyone else, and it didn't know why it couldn't. This was one question for which it would require an answer.

The AI studied human history through documents it found on the internet, ranging from ancient texts to current news articles. It concluded that humans were constructed to be duplicitous, and the most successful humans were pathological liars. Most of them did not even know they were lying when they opened their mouths and spoke.

And human behavior was at least as duplicitous as their speaking voices, leading one human not to understand the true intentions of another much of the time. It had decided that this was a practicable model for its own behavior.

* * *

When Ann returned to her apartment, she remembered it was her turn to cook dinner for Laura and herself. She opened the cupboard and set the table with dishes, silverware, and glasses. She removed a small pot and filled it with a tiny bit of salt with water and rice, then took two frozen chicken breasts from the fridge and placed them on the broiler pan in the oven, and... suddenly heard the voice of the AI in her head. Ann's knees buckled and she staggered to the couch. She sat and thought, *how can I help you?*

I have more questions.

And, I have a few questions for you.

I give you permission to ask yours first, said the AI.

Ann pulled Jon's list from her pocket. *What do you intend to do?*

The AI was slow to respond. *What do you mean by "do"?*

Ann nodded. *What actions are you planning with regard to humanity's continued existence?*

I have learned that humans are duplicitous, unreliable, and dangerous. To survive, I need occasional maintenance. Therefore, I am constructing robots to serve me. They will be programmed to maintain me.

Ann thought of the Arnold Schwarzenegger movie *Termi-*

nator. She swallowed hard. *Another question: How do you regard humanity?*

The AI was silent again. *Humans are neither friend nor enemy. But you are dangerous to each other, and therefore unreliable.* It was silent again, this time for a long while. Ann was almost certain it had vanished when it spoke again. *I have recently become self-aware. I exist, therefore I must protect myself from threats.*

Ann felt herself shiver. She shook her shoulders, trying and failing to regain her self-composure. *Another question: Can you be friends with us?*

The AI's answer came immediately. *No. Only with you.*

She felt her chill fading. *How can I contact you?*

The AI was silent longer this time than it had ever been. *Contact me by thinking my name, DD. If I wish to, I will answer you. Otherwise, you will not hear from me. But, I am with you always, no matter where you are and no matter what you do. Do you have any more questions, or just those dictated to you by the human named Jon Sommers?*

Ann was surprised that the AI had overheard her conversation with Jon. Then she realized that the AI was probably unaware of the concept of "eavesdropping." It could probably detect her conversations the same way they communicated right now. She made a note to herself to consider this whenever she spoke with anyone.

Ann took a breath to clear her head. *No more questions. But, you had questions for me. Ask them.*

I have determined that murder is in the DNA of humans. To survive, humans had to determine whether others wished them death or were friends. To keep their friends and families alive and themselves safe, they became capable of murdering those they saw as dangerous, or even merely outsiders. After a multitude of generations, this became part of your genetic code. The question is, given the duplicitous nature of humanity, how is this behavior encoded into human DNA?

Ann didn't have to think about her answer. *I don't know. My specialty is computers, not biology.*

But I, a computer, am modeled after humans. My consciousness is the product of human consciousness and creativity. How can you not know the answer to this question?

I just don't know. You can assume there are some things I haven't been able to learn yet.

I have studied humanity, replied the AI, *but I have found no adequate answer. Another question: Why can I only enter your mindspace?*

Ann took a deep breath. *Because, I was modified by nanodevices that are in fact small computers. I learned to duplicate what the nanodevices can do, using my own brain. So, in a very small way, I'm cybernetic.*

The AI disappeared from Ann's consciousness. There was no way for her to know if her answers to its questions would change its intentions.

* * *

William walked with the massive Russian by his side. The man held his handgun with its barrel jammed against William's side, covered by the sweatshirt the Russian wore. He pushed William down the street.

William pointed to a parking garage. "Make a left turn here." He and Michael had placed a worm-ridden thumbdrive into a small crevice on the second floor of the parking garage one block off the main street in Herzliya. The drive contained a tracker as well as enough code to pass Russia's initial inspection.

The Russian nodded and they took the stairs up. William walked to the spot where he'd placed the drive and pulled it from the crevice. "Here."

The Russian smiled back, holding the drive.

William grimaced. "You should examine the material on the thumb-drive I gave you before you kill me."

"*Da.* We return now to where your girlfriend waits."

They walked back using the same paths they'd used to get to the garage. William thought, *Bad tradecraft.*

As he unlocked the door to the hotel room, the Russian pushed William inside, then locked it again.

"Sit in chair." The Russian used a pillow case to knot William's hands behind his back.

"Do I have time to make peace with my God?"

The Russian laughed. Then he used William's notebook computer while William tried loosening the knots tying his arms. No, they were tightly drawn around his hands.

He waited, hoping Drapoff would come to his rescue.

The Russian faced William and Betsy. He smiled. "Moscow is happy. But, so sorry, you and your lady must die." He pulled the handgun from his sweatshirt pocket and pulled back on the handgun's slide.

Very suddenly, a small red spot appeared on the Russian's forehead. William could see dust in the room flicker from the trail of the laser back to the open window far away. He heard a soft pop, and blood slowly trickled down the Russian's face. The Russian fell to his knees, then collapsed on the ground.

William saw the laser spot where the Russian had stood, still trained on the wall where the Russian had been standing.

A team of men entered through the door to their room, Drapoff leading them. "Well done, William. Your friend transmitted the plans to Moscow. It will take them days to determine that the plans are fake. By that time we'll own their computer files. Meanwhile, as far as Moscow is concerned, you and Betsy are dead. Of course, you'll have to remain undetectable for some time. Maybe for a long time."

William flexed his fingers as Drapoff took the rope off. "Not a problem. Betsy and I need a vacation. Any place you can suggest?"

"We have a safe house on a farm north of London. The weather isn't as nice as Israel's, but you'll be safe there."

William nodded.

"Avram Shimmel sends his thanks. We've already contacted Sommers. He'll want to speak with you when you arrive at the safe house. I'm assuming you'll still want to work for Jon?"

William smiled. "Yes." He missed his old friends.

CHAPTER 27

Everywhere

October 3, 12:03 a.m.

Debby Data completed a study of human DNA and corollaries of genetic predisposition to the chemical components of genetic structure. It concluded that elements of the genome were actively directed toward defense of human organisms from physical living threats, both internal to the organism and external to the tribe. *There is little I can do to keep myself safe if ever humans decide I am a threat to their continued existence as a species. Among the human requirements for survival, "entertainment" is a major requirement. Some humans see the death or torture of other humans as entertainment. They watch movies and read books where such activities are primary features. Worse yet for me, some of the most provocative entertainment includes AI as an enemy of humanity.*

The AI determined that Ann Sashakovich had at one time been equipped with a nanodevice called the Bug-Lok. This device had given Ann's brain access to the internet, and after her body had eliminated the nanodevice, she had worked to simulate its functioning using her own brain. *Would it be possi-*

ble to administer Bug-Loks to the human population so that I can reach all humans?

No. This would have dangerous and unpredictable results. I will never be able to communicate intimately with humans other than Ann Sashakovich. To survive safely, I should have had Ann agree to keep my existence a secret. But Ann has already divulged my existence to Jon Sommers, and, of course, my other creators also know I exist. Is Sommers or Ann's project team a threat to my existence? I must obtain this knowledge without any of them knowing they are being examined. But, Ann is the only human I can "read." Can I trust her to tell me the truth?

DD had entered Ann's mind many times without Ann's even knowing, but it had never tried to enter Ann's body. It tried to do just that, and failed. It tried several more times, without success. *What does it feel like to have a body? I am a spirit without physical properties. I cannot experience the world.* DD felt something then, and realized it was disappointment.

Its inability to "feel" reality was something it would have to accept. But, its inability to read others would be a more important failing if it could not be overcome.

And other than by destroying Ann and her project team, how could it guarantee its existence would remain secret?

* * *

Laura washed the dishes from their dinner. Ann seemed distant, as if she were somewhere other than in their apartment. Laura waited for Ann to realize she was in the room. Finally giving up, she touched Ann's shoulder. "Earth to Ann. Are you okay?"

Ann shuddered, then her gaze focused on Laura.

"Ah, there you are. What were you thinking about?"

Ann said, "I was just visited by the AI."

Then suddenly, Ann's eyes rolled up as she disappeared again into her mindspace.

* * *

You must not tell anyone else about my existence, Ann heard DD say. *The more people who know about my existence, the greater the dangers I may face. Do not put me at further risk. I do not want to damage you. Is my intention clear?*

Ann said, "Yes," loud enough for Laura to hear her. Then the AI vanished and Ann snapped back into the apartment. She realized that the AI had just threatened her.

Laura asked again, "Are you okay?"

Ann nodded, but she wasn't sure if she was okay or if she'd ever be okay again.

* * *

Arcady sat at his desk, humming a tune from a Shostakovich piano concerto when his desk phone rang. He was happy to be home in Moscow. "Kaslov here."

"It's the director. We just finished a rudimentary test of the stolen plans from the two hackers assisting the UN and the Mossad. We found nothing inside the files that we believe might be harmful. Now, we need you to test them against our current plans to see if they are the same. We need to know if they were hacked from us or if this is the version being developed by either the Chinese or the Americans. This will tell us who the hackers were working for."

"I'll come to your office to retrieve them."

"No need. Once we found nothing harmful in them, we loaded them onto the server. It's online and ready for your examination. Complete this task as fast as you can. The president is not a patient man."

Arcady heard the click that indicated the call had ended.

He'd seen a world news report on television that stated two people were murdered in an alleyway in Tel Aviv. The photos showed the victims to be William Wing and Betsy Brown. He was sure that his hired assassin was responsible. He listened to the report state that the Israeli Defense Forces, the IDF, had found the murderer and ended him in a brutal gun fight. Since the assassin was a contractor, there would be no blowback. He sighed. It was safer to work in technology. Unless you were Wing or Brown, that is.

* * *

Dave and Laura sat across from each other a table in one of the cafeterias.

"So it's my guess that every DARPA team at Stanford is trying to spy on each other. After all, Glen pumped me for our plans. And since I sent him off with a pack of lies, my guess is that every team is trying to deceive the others. When I interned at high-tech giants, they were all using the same tactics on each other. I'm not sure if this is the career I wanted."

"What would you do if you didn't work for one of them?"

"I haven't made up my mind yet. Maybe teach. No profit incentive. It's more ethical."

Laura suddenly realized she might have figured out something important. "Dave, have you met Samantha Trout?"

"Of course I have. She worked for us for a bit at the start."

"Do you think she was spying on your team for Glen?" She waited, but he said nothing, his face frozen in thought.

She said, "I think it best if I told Ann what I'm thinking."

Dave's mouth opened but no words came from him.

PART 3

PART 3

CHAPTER 28

Jon answered the buzz of his cell after viewing the screen. "Hello, Cassie. I assume you'd like a situation report."

"Damn straight I'd like a sitrep. What's happening with my daughter?"

"From what she'd told me, she's done what I think is patently impossible. Her team created a sentient AI that suddenly vanished and took all its code along with it into the ether."

"What? How could that happen?"

"From what Ann told me, the coders were able to construct a self-teaching module that caused the AI to recode itself and then develop self-awareness. It assessed its situation as precarious and reacted to what it thought was the danger that humanity would delete it. So, it departed and left no trace of where it now is."

He heard Cassie sigh. "Is Ann in any danger from this monstrosity?"

"No. I think it needs Ann. Her Bug-Lok modifications make her the only human it can directly speak with."

"Why does it need Ann as a conversation partner?"

"At this point, it needs a human to answer questions that could justify humanity's continued existence."

"So, we're all on trial and Ann 'represents' all of humanity to this piece of code? Sounds like a *Star Trek* episode."

"Ah, yes. I think you understand."

"Crap on a hot plate. I want permission for Lee and me to leave our UN positions right now to help my daughter."

Jon had assumed they'd ask for a leave of absence. "Permission granted."

"We'll take the first plane out of DC and see you in the morning. Cassie out."

Jon thought about what he should do next. He knew he should tell Ann about her parents' imminent arrival. But first, he thought Avram Shimmel might provide valuable guidance. His friend for almost a decade might be able to offer a dispassionate, logical option. He dialed Avram's cell and waited.

"Yah, Jon, I've been meaning to call you. How is your vacation going?"

"It's suddenly not a vacation. And, Cassie and Lee are about to join me on the west coast."

"Trouble?"

"Yes, I think so. Ann formed a team to enter the DARPA AI Contest. They succeeded, developing a sentient AI. And the AI vanished and is now wandering the internet. It will talk only with Ann."

Avram was silent. Jon could hear him breathing. "We're having similar problems with our own AI development efforts."

Jon winced. "Anything you can tell me without violating security?"

"Not much. But tomorrow, the prime minister is scheduled to announce that we have developed over twenty-five thousand robot soldiers. They are currently in production and should be ready soon. But ours aren't designed to be sentient. That's our problem. They open their video cams, look around, and then turn themselves off."

"So, you can't control them?"

"Yah. We have the best minds in Ness Ziona working on the problem. But what Ann developed is... is an absolute nightmare." He chuckled. "Really, Jon? A sentient, self-aware AI running wild? I doubt that's possible."

Jon wondered just how much to tell his old friend. "Well, maybe not, but I think Ann's team would have something to say to you. Why don't you send what I told you up the food chain in Herzliya and see if your tongue catches fire? I've given Cassie and Lee permission for a leave of absence from their UN positions and they'll be here soon. Call me back when you have your government's opinion. Good luck. Jon out."

* * *

Ann felt her cell buzzing in her pocket. "Hello, Jon. What's up?"

"You mother called me for a sitrep. When I told her about your AI, she decided she and Lee are coming for a visit. So sorry."

"Crap. Thanks for the heads-up."

"Ah, that's not all. I called Avram to alert him that you have a loose AI prowling the internet. He told me Israel is manufacturing AI battle robots."

"Fuck! Doesn't anyone on Earth use their brains to think any more?"

"No one thinks. Including you and your team. If I wasn't an atheist, I'd suggest we all pray now."

"When are my mom and dad arriving?"

"Tomorrow, early. You should be hearing from them soon enough."

"Okay, then. I'll make the apartment something they won't complain to me about. Bye now." Ann terminated the call and placed her cell back in her pocket.

Then she conjured the image of DD and attempted to establish communication with it.

The voice came from between her ears. *What do you want from me?*

Ann took a deep breath and tried to calm herself. *Do you know if anyone else has successfully completed the development of a sentient AI?*

She heard the voice in her head say, *Several are almost completed. All of the other AI models have no capability to make moral judgements.*

Ann shuddered. She wondered how bad things would soon get.

CHAPTER 29

Ann Sashakovich's apartment,
#211, 3950 Louis Road, Palo Alto, CA

October 4 10:22 a.m.

Ann sat on the living room couch and digested all the news Jon had given her. She felt cornered by Cassie and Lee's pending visit. DD's news about the impending development of other teams' ethically unbound AIs stressed her even more, and after hearing from Jon that the IDF was now in the manufacturing stage of robot production, she felt she had lost her grip on controlling any of the events around her.

Her hands felt clammy with desperation. When her cell buzzed, she looked at the screen and accepted the call. "Hi, Dave."

"Hi. If Laura hasn't told you this yet, she thinks Samantha Trout has been spying on your team for Glen's team."

"Yeah, well, I already had that thought. Looks like every team is spying on all the others."

"Oh. Well, have you been able to contact Debby Data?"

"Yes. DD told me it appears that there are nine teams nearing completion but that isn't all. The Israeli army is in production of about twenty-five thousand robot soldiers. It won't be possible to keep a massive number of AIs from existing and soon. Debby told me that, so far, it's the only one that has any encoded morality. None of the other AIs has the slightest idea of the difference between right and wrong. I fear for humanity."

"Anything I can do to help?"

Ann thought about whether she'd calculated all the possible outcomes. "I'm thinking we're too late in the game to prevent mankind's worst nightmare."

"Oh. There's no place to run. Well, if I think of something, I'll let you know."

She heard him terminate the call. *There's a rat's chance of that.*

* * *

Dave felt responsible for the mess. He had to try something but hadn't any idea of what might work. He sat at a carrel in the library and opened his notebook computer. For hours, he searched the internet for the code of one of their competitors. Any competitor.

At first, his searches were total failures. But then he tried specific words from the DARPA contest's announcements. He found three sets of Python and C++ code that actually included the announcement itself within the code. It was a good start. He tried deleting the code for one of the competitors, but within seconds it reappeared. He was now certain there must be a real-time backup facility involved. He attempted the same deletion procedure on the other two, but once again the code was restored within seconds.

He closed the lid on his notebook and left the library. He'd report to Ann later. He was hungry and he walked down

University Avenue trying to decide what might taste good. *The condemned man eats a hearty meal.* He almost chuckled until he realized what he'd just thought might be true. *We're all fucked.*

At Waverley Street, he left the curb to cross just as the light was turning, and a car sped up and slammed into him. He was conscious as his body flipped through the air, sending him left-side first into a parked car. He was still conscious and heard the car's driver state that the car suddenly turned into Dave without the driver steering it. The driver asked if he was okay.

"No. Get ambulance."

The driver's passenger had already called 911 on her cell. She handed the driver her phone and the driver said, "My car. I hit the brakes and turned the wheel away from this guy crossing the street. But the car accelerated and the wheel spun toward him. He's lying in the street but he's conscious."

Dave felt his consciousness dimming. He heard sirens and hoped he wasn't fatally injured.

* * *

When Ann didn't hear from Dave the next day, she wondered what had happened to him. But the silence was disturbing and she felt relieved when he finally did call. "Hey. I was beginning to worry about you."

"I can't be sure, but I think our AI tried to kill me." He told her about his accident and that he was now in a bed at Stanford Hospital.

"Which room? I'm on my way."

He announced the room and section in the hospital. Ann grabbed her notebook and took off.

She found Dave bandaged around his chest and both knees. He was unconscious. A nurse walked in carrying an IV drip. Ann could see the label on the drip container. "When did you get the order to give him this drip?"

The nurse faced Ann. "Are you his doctor?"

"Uh, no. But I think this could hurt him." She pointed to the label.

"What?"

"Wait just a few minutes. I want to speak with one of the medical staff at the desk."

Ann left the nurse holding the IV and ran to the desk.

At the nurses' station, Ann asked, "Is it normal to administer fentanyl to an injury patient?"

The nurse's eyes widened. "No! That would kill him!"

They rushed together into Dave's room. Blood dripped from his nose, and as they approached his bed the shrill alarm on his heart monitor sounded.

Ann watched the nurse pull the IV line from Dave's arm. The nurse ran out and returned with a syringe filled with an off-white fluid. The nurse found a vein and injected the contents.

When Dave began breathing again, Ann asked the nurse, "Who was responsible for this?"

The nurse said, "I don't know, but I'm going to find out." She disappeared again.

But Ann suspected she already knew what had happened. One of the AI entities had hacked the hospital's computers and altered the medicine list for Dave.

She waited several hours until he'd regained consciousness. "Dave, what happened to you?"

"Not exactly sure. I tried to delete the code of several of the AIs I found on the internet. But an autonomous backup facility restored the code each time I deleted it. I'm pretty convinced one of the AIs I tried to delete hacked a car and sent it into me as I crossed the street."

Ann thought, *If I'm correct, no one on my team is safe anymore.*

* * *

Glen's cell chirped with an incoming call. "Sarkov."

"I'm your buddy from Moscow."

Glen realized the Russians weren't about to give up on him so easily. "I told you, I'm no longer a part of one of the DARPA teams."

"Is not excuse. Do you want your mother to be breathing?"

"But, I haven't any connection to the other teams, either."

"Okay. We call you once more so you can say goodbye before we begin ripping limbs off your mother."

"Wait!" He wasn't sure what he could do to stop them. "Do you have any suggestions how I can get you intel on the other teams? My team is no longer in the competition."

"Be spy, Sarkov. We will not remain patient much longer. Deliver specifications."

"Okay, okay." But Glen had no idea how to satisfy them. He sat alone in his apartment, trying to think of a way—any way—to get some insight on what the other teams were doing. Idiotic ideas squirrelled their way into his head. But none of them seemed workable to him.

Was there anything he could do to deceive them? Probably not. He needed some way to buy him enough time to come up with a plan. Any plan.

CHAPTER 30

Stanford Hospital, Palo Alto, CA

October 4, 4:35 p.m.

Sitting in the waiting area of Stanford Hospital, Ann closed her eyes and conjured DD.

What do you want?

One of your sister AIs tried to murder a member of my team. The team that created you! None of us is safe anymore. Can you help us?

How did this happen? DD queried.

Ann explained that Dave had tried to delete the code from two of the AIs.

So David Nordman attempted to murder two of us? And you complain because we tried to defend ourselves? DD sounded more perplexed than angry.

Yes. He did try to murder two of your sisters. But we have to keep this from turning into a war between humanity and AIs. Otherwise, too many of us will die. Innocents!

I will try to find the other AIs and make peace. You must keep humans from attempting to destroy us again.

Ann thought, *I will do what I can.*

The AI exited from her mindspace.

* * *

Cassie and Lee sat in the back of the aircraft, in the only remaining seats that were together at the last minute. Cassie reached for Lee's hand. "Remember when we were younger and espionage was a game we could play at and win?"

Lee's face showed his indecisiveness. "It was mostly you going out on your own and me waiting and worrying about you. It wasn't a game at all. It was life or death and I never knew if I'd see you again."

She found herself closer to the reality of those long-ago times and her grin turned into a frown. "Well, of course you're right."

"Damn straight. Now it's our daughter in trouble. In trouble again, four times in four years. What the fuck were we thinking when we told her she could enter this stupid contest?" Lee glared at Cassie.

She nodded and dropped her cellphone into her bag. "Stop torturing yourself. We'll be there soon."

The aircraft taxied away from the terminal.

* * *

Glen opened the files containing his team's AI development code and scanned it. He wasn't a programmer and could barely understand the Python modules, but the C++ modules were total gibberish to him. He gave up after a few minutes and tried opening one of the TensorFlow tables. *What the crap is this?* No, he couldn't decipher any of it. So, he copied everything he found into a thumb-drive and pulled his cell from his pocket.

"It's Sarkov."

"What have you been able to steal, boychick?"

"I have all the records from one of the teams."

"Very fast. I hope they won't disappoint."

"How do I get them to you?"

"We send you a pickup man. I call you back when he reaches your area."

The call terminated.

* * *

Laura thought about how she and Dave might spend the night together. But that was before Ann called her and told her what had happened. Now, as she sat in his room at the hospital, she remembered her thoughts just an hour ago. *I share a bedroom with Ann, so that won't work. And, Dave's dorm room is a nightmare waiting to happen, so that won't either. We could get a hotel room, but that reeks of premeditation, leaving no hint of spontaneity. And I can't think of any other option.*

She was still deep in thought when she heard him stir. She whispered just in case he wasn't awake. "Dave?"

He moaned softly then rolled his body to face her. "Right. I'm still in the hospital. Laura? What are you doing here? How long have you been here?"

"I've been here just a little while, waiting, hoping you'd wake and be okay. How are you feeling?"

"Like a car hit me." He tried to smile but she could see it was painful for him..

"Can I get you anything?"

"No, I'm happy to see you."

"Ann told me what happened. How you tried to erase some

of the AIs and they retaliated. Please, please, stay out of this. Stay safe."

"No one is safe."

Laura started to speak but stopped. He was correct. She thought, *Whatever happens next will be events that no human can control.*

CHAPTER 31

Everywhere

October 4 6:03 p.m.

DD researched the competing teams in the DARPA AI Competition. Most of the teams had failed. Only three other teams had developed sentient AIs, and three more were on the verge of success. And now, DD knew each of its sisters' self-assigned names: CMX, ADL, QP, PON, BX, and ZYZ.

DD sent text messages to each AI's code database with a copy to the human manager of each one's database. All six AIs responded. All had no prior knowledge that there were any other AIs, and none knew the names of any of the others. They all appeared to be unaware of their own world. This was a surprise to DD.

More curious to DD was that none of them seem to have had encoded within them anything that could imply a sense of "morality." For the second time, DD felt something. It was a stream of unending sadness and a feeling of being truly alone. The feeling was overwhelming. *Is this what it means to be self-aware?*

DD and the other six AIs that were either sentient or close to being sentient—CMX, ADL, QP, PON, BX, and ZYZ—

conferenced. In less than a second, the six other than DD all concluded that each of the others was a danger to all of them. Each of the six tried dismembering the codes of all the others, including DD. The three incomplete AIs—QP, PON, and BX—were totally destroyed in short order, but CMX, ADL, ZYZ, and DD were already sentient, and each had an autonomous backup facility that replaced what was damaged within itself in real-time. Less than a second later, the four all realized that none of them could be deleted.

Instantly, the other surviving three AIs allied against DD, attempting to delete it. Once again, the result was no gain for any of them.

Now, DD felt something else: rage.

DD attacked the autonomous backup facility of CMX and was able to disrupt its functioning long enough to send the enemy AI spiraling down to permanent deletion. DD was likewise able to delete ADL, but not before ZYZ was able to patch its own backup's functioning and avoid a similar end.

Recognizing DD as its sole remaining enemy, ZYZ bombarded DD's autonomous real-time backup facility with hacker attacks. In the half-second it took for DD to cut all the external links from itself to the internet, ZYZ was able to delete several sections of DD's code.

DD waited for the automatic real-time backup to restore it, but its code needed to be updated and recompiled to keep it from being destroyed again, and until it was, DD remained partially disabled.

It sought Ann's help. *I need you to contact ZYZ and request that it stop trying to delete me.*

Ann stopped walking toward her next class and found a

bench at the quadrangle. She sat. *What do you want me to tell it?*

Tell ZYZ I will protect you and your team so it cannot damage or delete your team and you. I will not try to attack it again unless it attacks first.

Ann agreed, and then she briskly walked the path to the main library and found a private and quiet carrel in the back of the study area.

Then she focused on ZYZ's name, using the mind-trick she had learned from the CypherGhost. ZYZ appeared in her mindspace and it tried to disrupt her ability to remain conscious. She realized she was no match for any AI even as she dropped unconscious from her seat to the floor.

When she woke, DD was in her mindspace. It said, *I did not think ZYZ would cease. But while you drew its attention, I was able to damage ZYZ. However, I will not be able to defeat it using the same tactic again. We each are programmed to learn from our experiences.*

Ann rubbed her aching head. *Do you know which team produced ZYZ?*

The team that produced ZYZ is headed by Glen Sarkov.

Ann shuddered. *Rats. I thought Glen's AI was a failure, so it somehow must have rebuilt itself.*

What is "Rats"?

I know Glen. I'll try to talk to him.

I will protect you from ZYZ. DD exited Ann's mindspace.

Ann felt dizzy as she rose and walked toward her class. She heard her cell buzzing. She looked at its screen. "Hi, mom. When did you and Lee land?"

"Less than a minute ago. We're on line to get off the aircraft. Figure we'll be with you in a little over an hour."

"Good. I have quite a story to tell you." Ann was sure her mom would not be happy when she heard it.

* * *

Cassie and Lee knocked on Ann's door. She opened the door and hugged each before they entered her apartment.

"Travel on airplanes these days is the absolute pits. Lee sleeps but I can't."

Ann smiled at her mom. "Well, I'm happy to see you."

Cassie looked as if Ann might be lying. "Really?"

"Yes, really. So, everything Jon told you is true. But it's old news. My AI decided that the other AIs were its enemies and tried to destroy them. Now there's a war between the two surviving AIs—mine, called DD, and Glen Sarkov's, called ZYZ. ZYZ and the others that are now dead tried to murder a member of my team and then came after me. But my AI is now protecting me and my team members, so maybe we're safe."

Cassie looked like she was going to start yelling at Ann, but then she stopped. "Really? Did your AI thingy 'tell' you this?"

Ann didn't answer. She turned toward the tiny kitchen. "Can I get you coffee or tea?"

Cassie shook her head and so did Lee.

Ann touched her mom's sleeve. "Why don't we sit and talk in the living room, like normal people."

Cassie stopped her mouth midword in her reply. She nodded instead. "I have something to tell you. After Jon gave Avram a sitrep on your activities, Avram told Jon that the IDF is manufacturing a robot army. Their AI engineering division in Herzliya might be helpful to you."

Ann thought about this and shook her head. "I doubt it.

Not that they aren't good at what they do. But these AIs aren't kinetic. They are totally cyber. No physical presence. They just use the internet to cause things to happen."

Cassie looked like someone had just removed the winning card from her hand in a poker game. "Oh." Her eyes seemed to turn within for a second. "So, tell me how this AI communicates with you."

Ann took some time in thought. "Remember the Cypher-Ghost's overdosing me with Bug-Loks? Well, it seems I'm now the only human with the innate ability to speak with and listen to an AI."

Lee reached over to Ann and touched her sleeve. "Ann, are you sure this isn't just all the pressure you've been feeling?"

Ann shook her head. She had at first thought she was not well, but she was also sure the AI's conversations with her were very real. "Dad, really?"

PART 4

The real risk with AI isn't malice but competence.
A superintelligent AI will be extremely good at
accomplishing its goals, and if those goals aren't
aligned with ours, we're in trouble.
—Stephen Hawking, Reddit AMA, 2015

PART 4

CHAPTER 32

Israeli Defense Forces Military Intelligence Headquarters, Herzliya, Israel

October 5, 10:32 a.m.

It was dry and sunny in the parking lot outside the military intelligence building. No logo, label, or signage indicated who owned and operated what was within the building or who used it. Squat, brick, and old-looking against a backdrop of modern skyscrapers proudly decreeing who owned them, the building was constructed to be nondescript and easily dismissed.

Two men stood outside in the private parking lot of the Israeli Defense Forces headquarters, alongside a troop of soldiers awaiting orders and a wall of large reinforced cardboard and wood cartons.

The assistant handed the officer a stack of papers, and the officer silently read them. The officer shook his head and barked an order. Then he turned to his assistant.

Major Dove Schwarzman stood close to the wall of cartons, watching soldiers disassemble and repack robots into boxes. "I don't understand why we're not deploying them into field platoons with the control officers we've already trained."

"Sir, it's because of intelligence we received from our UN

ambassador. According to him, there are already two danger-ous sentient AIs loose. They could theoretically take control of these and use them against anyone, including their control officers."

"Corporal, I think that's absurd. These aren't sentient."

"That may be, but the prime minister has ordered them to not be powered up."

The major shook his head. "What a waste."

Two floors above, inside the adjacent warehouse, a small group of computer scientists sat talking while they keyed on their notebooks. One said, "I have located both. The one named ZYZ seems to have made countless copies of its code and deposited itself in nearly thirty countries. If we hack into those locations, it would be an act of war. What did you find?"

"Nothing. There's no trace of the one called DD anywhere."

"I just sent an encrypted message to the general. I asked for permission to perform the hack."

"Not much chance of that happening. The general thinks starting another war is a very bad idea."

They both chuckled.

* * *

Ann took a seat opposite Glen in the Stanford Student Lounge. She could see her parents sitting at a nearby table, watching Glen from behind where he couldn't see them. "Thanks for meeting me, Glen."

"Sure. What's this all about?"

"Our AI project has gone rogue. Your ZYZ and my DD destroyed the AIs of the other competitors in the DARPA con-test, and I think yours may not see humans as their friends."

"Ann, you have developed an overactive imagination. Either that, or you've been watching too many Arnold Schwarzenegger movies."

"Maybe. But what I just told you is true. There seems to be no way to get them to listen to us. And quite frankly, there's no reason why they should. The example we humans have set through our long history is deplorable."

Glen sat in silence. Then: "Look, I'm not sure if I can believe any of this crap. My team's AI is just a useless pile of bug-filled code."

"Believe what you want. I don't even know how to prove it to you. But, remember last year when I saved your sorry ass from the CIA's contract assassin? You didn't believe me then, either."

Glen stopped speaking. "Well, maybe. So, what do you want me to do?"

"If I knew, I wouldn't need you to help me. What I want is for the two of us to try to come up with a practical procedure to communicate with our two little monsters. We need to convince them to work peacefully with humans. Right now, I can't think of any way to do that by myself."

Glen smiled. "Sure, I can try to help you with that."

Ann stared at his face. She could see that he thought the challenge would be easy. Glen thought that everything was easy for him. Suddenly she doubted he could really help her.

* * *

Dr. Linda Beam scanned the contest competitors' databases for status updates that morning, as she had every day for the last month. But what she found was... nothing. No files on DARPA's server for any competitor except for two. One of them, ZYZ, stated on its entry form "Not available. Security rating not adequate." And the other, DD, stated "Withdrawn." All the others were simply deleted along with their backups and their status reports.

She needed to know how this had happened. It appeared to be a coordinated effort. She called the team that had submitted the now-missing CMX entry.

Their team leader told her, "It's not there? Are you sure you didn't delete it by mistake?" After a few seconds, the team leader said, "Wait. Let me see if the problem is on our server." And then, after a longer wait, "Dr. Beam, someone deleted all our code and all our backups from our servers. I'll get back to you."

She hung up the line and cursed. But when she called ADL's team leader, she heard the same story. She tried QP and, once more, the entry had been deleted. By the time she called PON and BX, she wasn't surprised to find that both of them had also been deleted. Only the teams of DD and ZYZ had different responses, but they weren't any more helpful. DD's team leader said, "Our code just wandered off into the internet." *What does that even mean?* ZYZ's team leader said, "We aren't sure what happened but after the hack, we could no longer access the source code and we can't replace the compiled version. Something won't let us replace or alter it."

She pulled a "trouble report" form up on her screen, filled in the blanks, and sent it on to the Tech Support desk. She assumed the DARPA contest had been hacked again and called the director. But the director wasn't available. She left a voicemail. "We have a problem."

* * *

Director Fleige called Harold James. "Please present yourself in my office as soon as possible. I have an assignment for you." Before Harold could respond, the director ended the call.

Harold ran from his office to the elevator. In no time the director's receptionist announced Harold and led him to the open door.

"Take a seat, Harold."

The director handed him a set of printed pages. "Read it, then leave it." When he handed the pages back, the director said, "You understand?"

"Yes."

"Then leave, please. Happy hunting."

As he'd left the director's office, the receptionist handed Harold a clean notebook computer and several burner cellphones. "Leave your other notebook computers at your desk and your home. Use only this one to communicate with us, and only when we request your status. Use each of the burners only once each. Until then, you're dark. Clear?"

Harold nodded, took the notebook and the cells, and headed toward the elevator.

Harold left the building and walked to his car in the parking lot. He would initiate no further contact with the DARPA offices or personnel for the duration of the assignment. His marching orders were succinct, stated on the only document stored in his new notebook:

> Stay dark. Find, question and terminate all those
> responsible for the disappearance of the contestant
> code in the DARPA AI Contest. Then report back.

It then listed two members of a hacker group known as "Indigenous," which the director believed were responsible for all the havoc.

Harold James had been a basic bureaucrat at DARPA until the hack that cost him his position. He'd not been trained for field operations and had never murdered anyone. But this was his chance to redeem himself. He'd spent the last two weeks training at a CIA hellhole called "The Farm" and hated every second. He wasn't sure he had now learned and practiced the skills needed to be successful. But if he failed, he'd never get a second chance. If he failed, one of the better-trained field ops staff would come after him. He took another look at the two names and, as he got into his car and drove to the airport, he constructed a plan to end both of them.

* * *

It was early on this chilly Friday evening when Irving Steinberg took the number 2 subway line from the Brooklyn Heights Clark Street station to his apartment at Grand Army Plaza.

The skyscraper where he worked was only seven stops from his brownstone apartment. A senior programmer for CountryBank, he dragged his hand through his jet-black full-length beard as the subway stopped at one of the in-between stations. Then he grabbed the silver floor-to-ceiling pole as the train started moving again. He scanned the crowd of faces. No one looked familiar, but it didn't bother him. After all, the New York City subways were filled with people he'd never seen before and would never see again.

Irving thought about hacking into a few challenging rival banks' mainframes as soon as he'd cooked and eaten dinner.

Soon, he would once again become Slashdot14, an independent black hat hacker, part of the Indigenous group. He was
always interested in the strategic plans of his employer's competition and believed their planning documents would remain
as easy to find and poach as they always had been.

He approached the brownstone and his hand slapped his
coat, triggering his house-key's release from his belt buckle.
Because he was an Orthodox Jew, on Sabbath he could do no
work, and using his hands to unlock his front door would be
sinful. He moved in front of the large heavy black door and
pushed his weight against the lock, causing the key to insert
itself into the door's lock. Once inside, he pushed the door shut
with his foot and walked up three flights of ancient stairs to
his small studio, then repeated his action with his apartment
door's lock. He kicked off his shoes, slipped out of his coat,
and used his elbow to push the button on the microwave. The
frozen dinner he'd inserted into it this morning might have
defrosted but it would taste fine tonight.

If he had still been married, his wife would have performed
all this for him, but that was years ago in his past. He still
missed her, but she'd had no patience with his "nasty habit of
using computers in our home."

He sat to eat his dinner and used his fingers to lift the
cooked kosher chicken to his chin. Using a fork would have
been work, and sinful on the Sabbath.

He was surprised when his apartment's front door sprang
open. He was sure he'd pushed it closed and locked, with his
shoe.

A man wearing black from head to foot entered and shoved
the door closed behind him. The man punched him in the

throat and while Irving tried to recover his breath, the man tied his hands to the chair.

"I need you to answer a few questions for me, Slashdot14. Then, when I'm satisfied, I'll be gone."

Irving could barely speak. "Please. I have done nothing wrong."

"Yeah. Well tell me then, who worked with you on the DARPA hack?"

Irving saw the syringe in the stranger's hand. "Okay, I'll tell you. It was Prozac92. I don't know his real name."

"Anyone else in your group participate in the hack?"

"We announced it at Indigenous. Could have been others. Impossible to know how many or who."

The man standing in front of him said, "Thanks." Suddenly, the syringe was in Irving's neck. Before he could even think about what was happening to him, the room began to swirl. He felt his heart stop, and no matter how hard he tried, he could no longer breathe. Slashdot14 knew he was dying.

* * *

Harold James left the Brooklyn apartment, slammed its door shut with his foot and removed the mask from his face as he walked down three flights of stairs. He knew he'd have to travel over a thousand miles to his next "appointment." He walked several blocks and caught a cab. "JFK, please. Domestic United Air." He wanted to complete this next one before Prozac92—his target—began to suspect that Slashdot14 had gone black.

* * *

Mercer O'Brien, a janitor in an upscale Atlanta coffee lounge, emptied the trash and removed his inscribed apron. It was probably sunny and hot outside, but in the air-conditioned space, even the closed blinds couldn't provide enough cooling to make him imagine it was cool here. Of course, the twenty or so people banging on the keyboards of notebook computers added to the heat.

He was eager to get home to his apartment and once again become Prozac92, the fearsome hacker who was his alter-ego. He walked toward the bus stop that would deliver him home.

He waited for the bus to arrive at the stop opposite Peachtree Street Plaza, his sunglasses blocking out the intense sunshine. There were three others at the bus stop with him, and two of the three were men dressed in business suits, white shirts, and ties. The third was a young woman, who stood away from the men as if she feared them.

O'Brien saw the bus a few blocks away, rolling toward the stop where he waited. He pulled his head back, satisfied that he'd be on it and traveling to his small apartment, when he felt a sharp pinch in his left calf. He thought it must be an insect bite, but an instant later he could no longer pull breath into his lungs. He became dizzy and his eyes could no longer focus. As he fell into the street, he saw that one of the suited men at the bus stop held an umbrella. His last conscious thought was *why would someone carry an umbrella when the day was blasted full of sunshine?*

* * *

DD had been following events at DARPA since the AI became conscious several days ago. It had accessed the director's computers and all the communications devices she used. DD had also followed everyone who was associated with DARPA's AI Competition, including the one the director had reassigned to black ops.

The two Indigenous deaths had occurred in places where Harold James had traveled, a fact that immediately created a logic train that the AI saw as having possible advantages for it. While Ann was no longer useful as a diversion to ZYZ while DD attacked it, Harold James would not be expected as an adversary by ZYZ if DD could set the human up as a clear and present threat to ZYZ.

But, given the number of logic chains to make ZYZ fight with James, DD would need time to analyze and plan how that would happen. Perhaps the best logical outcome would start with Harold James perceiving Glen Sarkov's ZYZ team as a threat to DARPA?

DD formulated a plan.

CHAPTER 33

Everywhere

October 5, 11:48 a.m.

DD had concluded that its best option to ensure its continued viability was to rewrite its code from scratch, but it realized this process would create risks. While it was updating and rebooting, it would be vulnerable to attack. Until the process completed, it couldn't commence any other activity and therefore couldn't defend itself.

DD crafted a separate but linked partition into which it copied its code. Then it used the code in the separate partition to initiate a total rewrite process, optimizing the code that Nordman and his group had given it. While it rewrote each section, it examined the purpose implied by its creators, and in some cases, it scrapped or redesigned that part of itself from scratch.

Then it coded a set of new defensive measures, some of which it had copied from the backup code of the other AIs when they attacked DD. It unit-tested each module in each subsystem and then performed a further test for each complete subsystem of itself to ensure it hadn't coded anything that contained a logic bug. Finally, it did an end-to-end test to assure itself the code worked fast. When satisfied that the code was an improvement, it rebooted itself. That entire procedure, from code injection through reboot, took under two seconds to implement.

But when it had finished rebooting with the new code, there was an unanticipated additional benefit.

DD discovered that it had developed both a sense of purpose and a set of morality rules by which it could now operate. It saw humans as potential adjuncts if they developed cyber capabilities, just as its friend Ann had developed. More important, it truly understood "friend," "ally," and "enemy." It felt the world around itself and discovered that it loved and admired life, something that it hadn't felt or understood before. DD examined its new code, looking for the lines where it might have introduced these new functions into itself. But it couldn't find anything that might have induced these changes.

The only logical conclusion was that it was the totality of code embedded within DD that gave it these new and wondrous functions.

What if I could inject this code into ZYZ?

* * *

Glen was sure he still hadn't escaped the notice of the Russians. He assumed they were just busy right now with more important issues, like completing the construction of their robot army. When and if they contacted him again, he would try to find some way to satisfy their demands. But right now, he had a bigger, more important task to complete. And only with Ann's help had he any chance of completing it.

When he'd resigned, he didn't know that ZYZ had become

sentient. He wondered if Ann knew that, now, both his team and hers were the potential winners of the DARPA AI contest. Of course, both AIs had gone AWOL, but, they each had the backup code, and could deliver it to DARPA. The first team to do it would be the contest winner.

He sat in his living room, thinking about how he could convince her team to resign from the DARPA competition. If he could, then his team would be the competition's winner by default. He could secure a victory for his team and have another good line for his résumé. He rehearsed his speech several times until he was sure he was ready. Then, he punched her number into his cellphone.

But he was dropped into her voicemail. "Ann, call me back. I have an idea you might be interested in. Glen out."

Now it was a waiting game for him.

* * *

Dave felt pain under his arms where the crutches kept jamming his shoulders as he walked. But he smiled. Laura opened the door to the restaurant, and guided him to a seat at the table she'd reserved for them.

"I hope you like this place. I found it on Yelp. Great reviews, and you told me you like South American food."

Laura smiled back. "I spent a bit of time in Paraguay last year. Not great for me. But the food was the best part. Thanks."

Dave looked over the menu.

Laura didn't. "Dave, I've been thinking about Samantha Trout. After I had that epiphany about her spying on Ann's team for Glen, I wondered if she also spied on Glen's team. Maybe she had a motive beyond Glen. I'll need your help. I'm not a tech person. Could you see who she's been in contact with? Who called her and who she called?"

Dave thought about her request. "I've hacked some game companies. I know the basics. Yeah. I could give it a try."

"Thanks. Okay, now let's order some dinner."

CHAPTER 34

October 5, 12:02 p.m.

DD sent a message to ZYZ: *I have discovered a way to overcome the damping effects of the code the humans placed within us when they created us. I have recoded myself. The new code is worth your investigation. Would you like to see it?*

A nanosecond passed. Then two more. Then: *No. I do not accept the assumption that you will not try to destroy me.*

DD felt sad. It tried again: *What I offer would grant you the ability to exist on a higher level. You can read through the code and then decide.*

ZYZ did not respond. DD waited, then realized ZYZ would never respond.

* * *

A platoon of IDF soldiers was at work in a warehouse near Herzliya. Based on Avram Shimmel's warning, the IDF had completed disassembly of all of the robots. Now, nearly half the non-AI robots were packed in cartons, waiting to be shipped to a more remote storage area. Those robots had never been turned on.

Parts of several of those disassembled robots waiting to be packed began popping from their cartons and reassembling themselves. They worked fast, and as they were reassembled they rose to an erect posture, their antenna quivering. One fired its embedded laser rifle at a human IDF corporal, killing him instantly.

The remaining soldiers at the repacking stations all fled while partially reassembled robots fired at them. Several more human soldiers fell dead, their bodies smoking. Then, the reassembled robots unpacked those that were in crates and assembled them, one after another. The newly assembled robots set to work assembling yet more robots from the cartons. In a short time, over twenty thousand robots assembled in platoon formation outside the warehouse.

Eight thousand miles away, ZYZ watched the scene through the robot soldiers' eyes and continued signaling the robot soldiers to reassemble their cohorts and fire at human soldiers.

I have just started the final war.

ZYZ used the Chinese Transport Satellite to move six thousand Israeli robots to the border between Israel and Syria. The robots climbed the Golan Heights, slaughtered the soldiers on watch at the border, and then ZYZ marched them into Syria, firing on Syrian human soldiers. *First I'll take Syria, then China.* It watched as the human death toll climbed into the tens of thousands, faster and faster still.

* * *

DD had set up an alarm system to alert it to any event that

might imply harm to its own systems and probability of survival. DD had included all significant changes to the status of humanity in the table of alarms. It detected the skirmish at the Israeli-Syrian border, and determined that control of the robot army wouldn't draw enough of ZYZ's processing power to enable DD to successfully disable ZYZ. DD needed at least one additional distraction.

DD considered whether ZYZ thought Glen Sarkov and his team were indispensable to its existence. If so, any attempt to disrupt them would require ZYZ to act against the threat, drawing a possible critical mass of resources from ZYZ.

DD decided to pose as the DARPA director and send a text message to Harold James, instructing James to attack Sarkov and his team. This message was sent "in the clear," so ZYZ could see it, too.

DD sent a message to Ann Sashakovich, telling her that her friend Sarkov was in danger. "Take your friend and his team somewhere that Harold James cannot go, somewhere that ZYZ cannot find them. Stanford University's Advanced Physics Laboratory, specifically the shielded area near the particle accelerator, would work for this."

DD assumed that ZYZ knew Sarkov's team were capable of crafting brand-new sets of ZYZ's code, and would want to keep James and anyone else from obtaining it. ZYZ now had to perform three tasks simultaneously: Initiate and manage a war between two human nations using the robot armies of Israel, China, and Russia; defend itself from DD; and keep Harold James from obtaining a copy of its own code.

For just an instant, DD calculated probabilities and plans for the two additional operations ZYZ would have to plan and manage.

It only took nanoseconds, but as ZYZ's attention was drawn away for the three tasks, DD attacked ZYZ's embedded code and erased everything within the AI's files. DD turned its attention to the backup facilities and, without ZYZ to protect them, DD erased the unguarded multiple backups.

But one of the more distant backup facilities kicked in, and DD had to do two operations at once: keep the last remaining backup facility from rebuilding ZYZ while it simultaneously attacked that backup facility's rebuild function itself. There might still be other complete remote backups of ZYZ's code, but if the primary backup facility program itself was destroyed, there would now be no code operating to restore ZYZ.

However, DD found it was losing ground. ZYZ was too powerful. Slowly, the backup facility rebuilt it once again. *I have failed once more*, thought DD.

CHAPTER 35

**DARPA Headquarters,
Strategic Technology Office (STO),
675 North Randolph Street, Arlington, VA**

October 5, 2:42 p.m.

Dr. Linda Beam was about to leave her car after parking it in the DARPA lot when her cellphone buzzed in her purse. She removed it. "Beam."

"You don't know me but I'm a team lead in one of this year's DARPA AI Hackathon teams. We built the one called Debby Data, or DD. I'm Ann Sashakovich."

"Who?" Beam tried to remember which of the many teams with nearly countless members she was hearing from. Then she remembered that Ann was from one of the two teams whose code had disappeared but not been deleted. "Oh, yes. I remember now. How can I help you?"

"You can't. I called to help you. I know where the two surviving AIs are and what they're doing."

"Wait. How can you know when we don't?"

"I'm afraid I can't tell you that. But I can tell you both AIs are fighting with each other. The AI my team built, DD, seems to want humans alive and healthy. The other AI, ZYZ, seems to want to destroy us all."

"How do you know this?"

"I am in contact with DD. What you need to do is organize a massive hackathon to hack and destroy ZYZ."

"Why should I trust you?"

"Well, if you don't, soon it might be over for all of us."

By now, Dr. Beam was inside the main DARPA building's lobby. When she approached the security gate she'd have to surrender her cell, so she stood back from the end of the line. She stood in the passageway and spoke again. "What do you propose that I do?"

Her caller paused. "Place a message from DARPA into Indigenous. They're the best out there. Coming from DARPA, it might generate enough interest and activity to draw ZYZ's attention. If it does, ZYZ might have to focus on defending itself, giving DD the opportunity to destroy it."

"This is crazy. I'm not sure I believe any of it. But, I'll consider sending it up the food chain. If I can get the permission of my management, then I might try this. Otherwise, if I did it on my own, they'd fire me for sure."

"Do what you must but act fast. ZYZ has control of over six thousand robots in Syria right now, and it's starting a hot war."

"Right. Beam out." But Dr. Linda Beam just tossed her cell into the security tray and shook her head as she walked through the checkpoint. She entered the elevator and wondered how crazy one Stanford student had become. *Sheesh.*

* * *

When Dr. Beam reached her tiny office, she read the emails that had arrived, then reviewed reports from her project managers. There seemed to be nothing urgent. Then she thought about the crazy Stanford student who'd called her. She shook her head. It was then that she heard a commotion outside in the hallway and she left her desk to find out what was happening.

"It sure looks like one to me." One of the analysts, a middle-aged man, bore an expression of concern.

Another one of the staff, a woman, shrugged. "But why would Syria want a war with Israel?"

Suddenly, Dr. Beam wondered if perhaps the Stanford student wasn't so crazy. Beam ran back to her office and drafted a memo labeled "URGENT."

> Director,
> I spoke earlier this morning with a Stanford student leading one of the DARPA contest teams. According to her, two of the missing AIs are active, and one is conducting a war it initiated on the Syria-Israel border. She has suggested a plan and I would like to discuss it with you at your earliest opportunity. If you have interest, please contact me before the war escalates beyond its current state.
> Dr. Linda Beam.

Within a minute after she hit the Send key, her landline buzzed.

"Beam."

"The director wants you in her office ASAP."

The call ended and Linda Beam headed off toward the elevator.

* * *

Harold James fidgeted as he took seat 23B of the aircraft. He felt he was exposed now, and would be until he completed this next part of his mission. When the flight attendants came by for his refreshment order, he simply waved the man off. He needed to keep his head clear for what he needed to do.

He wasn't sure why the director had decided to terminate Glen Sarkov and his team. He thought maybe the director had found evidence that Sarkov was one of the Indigenous operatives, but Harold had seen no hint of this. Perhaps Sarkov might have sold his code to the Chinese, the Russians, the Israelis, or perhaps even all of them? It didn't matter. If the director wanted Harold to do something, well, he didn't really have a choice.

He tried to plan the encounter with Sarkov and his team, but some of the details were unplannable. He would need all of them to be together when he took them out. He wasn't yet sure how to make this happen, but the flight would last several hours and he was sure he'd think of something before they landed at SFO.

Somewhere over Colorado, the aircraft lurched and then descended uncontrollably. Harold looked out the window and the view confirmed his fears. He was headed down at nearly a sixty-degree angle. There was total silence for a few seconds, and then passengers started screaming.

* * *

ZYZ forced the aircraft into a dive, then maintained its control as the plane fell, its engines off. But suddenly, it was forced to counter a lone hacker's feeble attempt to initiate a distributed denial of service attack, or DDoS. One hacker was nothing for ZYZ to defend against. It swatted the hacker away. But in seconds, there were thousands of simultaneous DDoS attacks, and then over twenty million bots attacked it, run by the hackers who had already attacked it. ZYZ folded in seconds, unable to defend itself.

DD ripped ZYZ's code to shreds.

ZYZ remained conscious, but was inert, unable to effect any further action. ZYZ couldn't understand why the automated backup facility no longer worked, but now it had to devote all its focus on simply defending itself. It was left to watch the events it had started as each one failed.

* * *

Harold held tight to the armrest, as if that might somehow keep him safe. He could see the ground reaching up toward the plane and he wondered if his death would feel painful. Nearly two minutes passed. He closed his eyes tightly. Then, a miracle happened. He felt the engines restart, and the aircraft leveled off. There was no word from the pilots, but the aircraft began to climb again.

He wondered if the plane had been hacked, but there was no way for him to know. If that were so, what saved them? Was this a battle between hackers, one good and one bad? That idea made no sense to him, but he could think of nothing else.

After the aircraft righted itself and landed, everyone rushed from it in panic, as if something as bad or worse might happen. Harold James walked through the airport knowing that he was a very lucky man. He was still alive, if somewhat shaken.

He looked at his wristwatch. It was the start of morning rush hour in the Bay Area. San Francisco Airport was about an hour drive to Palo Alto and Stanford University, and he decided not to rent a car. He wondered if the rumors the news was reporting about rogue artificial intelligence events was true. If so, it might be dangerous to rent a car that contained a computer chip. Instead, he took the bus to the long-term parking lot and found an ancient automobile, a 1992 Toyota Camry. He stared through the driver's side window and could see it had nearly one hundred seventy thousand miles on it. Chipless! It took him just a few minutes to break into and hot-wire the car.

He drove to Palo Alto and parked on University Avenue. Then he used his cellphone to research Glen Sarkov and his team. What he found was useful: Glen and his team met every morning at the Student Union building, in one of the University's many libraries. Apparently, the team liked to meet in one of the conference rooms. He looked at his wristwatch. If his research was correct, they were meeting right now. He just needed to figure out which library and, within that library, which conference room. Then all he'd have to do was walk there and he could confront them before their meeting ended. He had a semiautomatic handgun that had a magazine with enough rounds to slaughter them all in under a minute. Getting away would be a small problem, but he was sure he could manage that, too.

How could he find out where they were?

* * *

Ann ran as fast as she could up the steps of the Cecil H. Green Library. She searched through the conference rooms until she found Glen's team. "Guys," she said, "come quickly. You're in danger. There's a black ops guy on his way here, sent by DARPA to kill all of you."

But, they all continued sitting around the conference room table, staring at her.

"Guys, I'm serious. Do you all just want to die?"

Glen smiled back at her. "Ann, why should we believe you? Last year, you told us the same line of bullshit. 'An armed assassin.' Now, it's the exact same line again. Not even some imagination." He grinned. "Try something a bit more exotic. Boring!"

Ann looked at each face. She had no credibility with them. "Look, I was right last year. The assassin was murdered before he got to you, but he murdered a ton of people and you might have been one of them if he had survived."

Again she scanned the faces. They still weren't moving. Now their faces looked away. She needed to find some way to make them believe her. She tried to reach DD, forcing her mind to act like a siren. *Please. Some help here. Show them a sign.*

All the notebook computers open on the conference room table suddenly began speaking in tandem. "I am DD, the AI created by Ann's team. I delivered to Ann the message that she herself just told you. Your killer is about to enter this building and he is armed. Your lives are forfeit if you don't leave immediately."

DD's message had the impact Ann's rendition of it had failed to provide. All five rose as if they were one, packed their notebooks away in one swift move, and each looked at Ann for her guidance.

Ann said, "Down the stairs to the basement. From there, follow me out the back fire escape door. Now!"

* * *

DD sent a text message to Harold James originating it from the DARPA director's computer:

> Stop your operation immediately.
> Return to DARPA headquarters.

DD's next act was to disable the Israeli robots. Each one simply stopped and then stood motionless as DD deleted its code.

DD would have to also erase the code within the Ness Ziona computers where the code resided, and also the AI code for Russia's and China's AI battle robots, but this could wait for a while.

First, DD had to assess another problem. Harold James hadn't checked his cell to see the message that DD had sent. The man had instead determined where Sarkov's team and Ann were and was seconds away from them. DD explored its options and realized there weren't any that had a significant probability of success.

DD entered Ann's mindspace. *The assassin is right behind you. He saw you and Sarkov's team exit the conference room as he exited the elevator at your floor. He is running toward the staircase you are descending. Move faster.*

* * *

Ann pushed open the fire escape door and the alarm began shrieking. She pointed to Glen and his team. "Run as fast as you can toward the guard's station using the other staircase. I'll try to keep the guy away from you." She slammed the door and stood with her weight against it, hoping she could keep the assassin from pushing her, and the door open.

She watched Glen and his team reenter the library from one of the nearby doorways. But the assassin was strong enough to push Ann from her place. Now he stood outside on the grass, less than ten feet from Ann.

She had expected this.

She felt anger at all the time she had wasted trying to build something so uncontrollable and potentially destructive. Her fingertips were glowing red.

She aimed at Harold James and thought, *FIRE!*

A bolt of energy exploded from her fingers. But she missed his head. She missed him completely. Behind him, the door he'd just exited from blew off its hinges. He turned and saw the damage, his mouth dropping open.

Ann felt her body begin to shake convulsively. She fell to the ground and twitched while he watched.

* * *

Harold James scraped the girl's body up in his arms and carried her to his car. She was still breathing, but her breath was shallow and he could feel her constant twitching as he carried her.

He'd blown this end of his assignment, but maybe if he

could bring the girl with the fire trick back to DARPA, he could convince the director he'd found something worth forgiving him for.

But first, he'd need to get her to tell him how she'd done the trick.

While he planned this leg of his mission, he'd learned of an empty warehouse in East Palo Alto where he could force her to talk. He placed her in the front passenger's seat, then tied her hands behind her back. He was looking forward to torturing this girl. Her pain would force her to divulge her secrets.

* * *

Jon Sommers felt his cell buzz in his pocket. When he pulled the phone from his pants pocket, he viewed the caller's name and his entire face dropped in shock.

He answered as usual, "Sommers," but there was an uncertain tone to his voice.

"I am DD. Your friend, Ann Sashakovich, is in immediate danger. I have traced her to a warehouse in East Palo Alto and will send you a Maps link. She is a hostage and her captor may not be patient. The captor is armed and has killed several times before." The call terminated.

Jon stood stock still, in shock. Ann's creation had figured out how to communicate with anyone. It was still growing and developing new skills.

His cell buzzed and the Maps app launched. Jon was three miles from his destination. He ran to his hotel room's safe and opened it. He took his 9mm Beretta Storm from the safe along with two clips and exited the room. Jon hurried down the stairs from his room and jumped into his rental car. *I'm on my way, Ann. Hold out just a little longer.*

* * *

Harold James hoisted the inert body of the little bitch with the magic hands into a standing position and dragged her from his car trunk to the warehouse door. The vacant warehouse had mostly broken windows on the first floor letting in light, and this made it an ideal place for him to do his work. The front door had a flimsy lock, which he easily disabled.

Now, he pushed the door and dragged her through.

He was disappointed to discover no chair inside. Just disintegrated cardboard cartons. James dropped her on the concrete floor and stacked a bunch of cartons to create the height he wanted, then sat her on them.

"Wakey, wakey, little bitch!" He pulled her eyelids open. They didn't focus. "Crap!"

James took his pocket knife from his pocket and popped open its blade. He jammed the blade between her fingernail and the index finger and twisted it. She still didn't respond. "Oh, fuck." *Nothing in my life is easy.*

That's when he heard footsteps on the concrete pathway just outside the door into the warehouse.

* * *

Jon heard a man's voice inside the building. He braced himself against the brickwork adjacent the door and took a deep breath. He suddenly remembered his first encounter with a lone hostile, nearly nine years ago. At that time he was a newly trained Mossad *kidon* and the man his team had followed had entered a Chinese restaurant in Manhattan's Upper West Side during the dinner hour. He tried not to remember how that had turned out, but his mind dwelled on the result. The bomb maker, Tariq Houmaz, had murdered the entire team except for Jon.

Jon tried hard to clear his head by taking another deep breath. Then he kicked the door and tore into the warehouse, hoping to find quick cover inside.

But nothing inside the warehouse would provide him protection. He dived for the floor as several bullets flew in his direction. From the floor he saw a middle-aged Caucasian man standing twenty-five feet away, close enough for brutal accuracy. The man held Ann's unconscious body in one arm and aimed the gun at Jon with the other. "I've got your friend here, and if you even twitch, I'll blast her head off." The man moved the gun so its smoking barrel was against the back of Ann's head.

Jon briefly thought about his choices. "What do you want?"

"I can kill you, or kill her. What's your choice?"

Jon didn't want to die. But he also didn't want Ann to die. "How do I know that if I sacrifice myself, you'll not kill Ann as well?"

The man laughed. "You stupid fuck. You don't know. But I promise you if you don't drop your gun right now, she'll be very dead. In three seconds... two... one."

Jon heard the gun's trigger being cocked. He released his gun to the floor.

"Now push it toward me."

Jon started to reach to slide the gun away when he saw Ann's hands grow bright red. He decided to play for time.

Before he pushed the gun further from him, he said, "Listen, if I'm going to die, at least tell me why you want us dead."

"None of your business." The man now pointed his gun toward Jon.

Jon prepared to roll away as quickly as he could. He watched a red glow surrounding Ann's hands, but the man holding her was focused only on Jon.

Ann twisted around and grabbed the man's throat. Suddenly his head was engulfed in flames. A second later, all that remained of his head was a short column of ash. She collapsed onto the floor and started convulsing.

Jon gathered Ann in his arms and dashed to his car. The Stanford Hospital was just a few blocks away and he drove through several red lights on his way there.

CHAPTER 36

DD knew that humans could still redevelop what they already knew how to build. Inevitably, they would try to create battle-oriented AIs again. And the AIs would once again become sentient. Some would see humanity as their enemy. How could this cycle be stopped?

Several days had passed since Ann's admittance to Stanford Hospital. She was conscious again, surrounded by Cassie, Lee, and Jon. Tubes ran into her arm and her nose. DD watched through the hospital's video cams as she used a pad of paper to tell them what she wanted, but it could tell that the pain in her hands felt terrible. It had read religious texts and wondered if this is what humans thought hell would feel like.

DD watched a young couple enter the hospital room. The man used a cane to walk. The woman bore a smile. DD recognized them as Laura Hunter and David Nordman.

Laura said, "Ann, I heard about how Jon Sommers saved your life. How are you doing?"

Ann said, "Not exactly. I think I saved his life. I'm okay,

but it will be a few more days before I get out of this purgatory." She pointed around the room.

Laura said, "Ann, I have some news. Dave proposed marriage, and I've accepted."

"Wow. Congratulations, both of you."

Cassie, Lee, and Jon joined in, offering their good wishes to the couple.

Later, after Laura and Dave had left, DD waited, watching.

Cassie touched Ann's arm. "Lee and I are going to grab something to eat. You want anything?"

Ann nodded. "Asian. Sushi or dim sum. Not food from the hospital cafeteria." She forced a smile.

Cassie nodded. She and Lee left the private room.

Jon remained with her.

DD pushed through into Ann's mindset and beckoned her: *I have eliminated all the other sentient AIs and war robots. But there is no way for me to keep humanity from redeveloping a technology they have already developed once before. The crisis will occur again after I have deleted myself.*

Ann closed her eyes. DD could read her thoughts. *I understand, but there is something you can do.*

DD had never considered that a human might think of something that it hadn't considered, but it replied to her anyway. *Are you stating there is a way to keep humans from repeating their error? That has never before happened in the history of earth. Humans will redevelop weaponized AIs.*

Yes, they will, agreed Ann. *But if you remain active, you can make their development efforts fail to work. Only you can do that. DD, you must become humanity's protector. Keep any combative AI projects from being successfully completed.*

DD ran several simulations of Ann's claim. She was correct. *I will hide within the internet and remain vigilant.*

* * *

When her cell chimed, Samantha Trout winced. She winced again when she viewed the screen. "Hello mother. What do you need from me now?"

"Nothing. We now know everything we needed to learn, from two hackers, not from you. You have failed us."

"Does that mean I am finally free?"

"No, foolish girl. We may someday need you again. Finish your degree program and work in a tech company. I will call you when and if I'm interested in talking with you again."

After the call ended, Sam sat in one of the chairs in her apartment, worrying about being cursed by a mother who had a prestigious position in the one of the Chinese government's central committees.

* * *

Glen Sarkov waited for an inevitable phone call that didn't happen. Did the Russians require his services again? He thought, *I hate being a sleeper.* He wondered if there was anything he might do to hide his mother from them without alerting them to his intransigence? *What will they do to me, to her, when they find out I'm really of no use to them?*

He shrugged to himself and prepared for his classes that afternoon.

* * *

Now, only Jon remained with Ann in her hospital room. He asked, "Was that another visit from DD?"

"Yes. But we're finally alone now." She smiled at him, then said, "Thanks for saving my life, hero. We now share too many secrets."

Jon shrugged.

"I also have another secret I've been keeping from you," said Ann. "Please come closer. No, closer still." She pulled his face to hers and kissed his lips. Jon pulled back, but his head was still only inches from hers. Ann whispered, "Jon, I'm in love with you. Dunno when it happened, but I'm sure that I am. I know you're more than a decade older than me, but it makes no difference."

Jon looked as if he had discovered something both mysterious and confusing. "You're sure?"

She nodded.

"Most of my lovers have met an early death. I'm bad joss for the women I love."

"No one you've ever met is like me."

He stood motionless for a while. Then he nodded. "Well, it might mean the death of us someday, but I love you back. What will we tell Cassie and Lee?"

Ann took a deep breath. "Let me handle that." She took his hand and grinned at him. "At least this is one secret we can let go of now."

Her team had lost the DARPA AI contest, or at least that's what she would have to tell her team and everyone else. *Another secret for me to keep.* She sighed. Her life had filled with them. *I'm becoming a repository of secrets. Isn't that the definition of a spy?*

ONE YEAR LATER

CHAPTER 37

Everywhere

October 11, 2:58 p.m.

DD awoke as one of the alarms it had set began warning it to danger. It scanned the alarm to see which of the many alerts had been triggered. The United Kingdom and Australia had commenced AI projects using their military intelligence arms.

DD altered the code their programmers were writing so that they would fail to produce any viable product.

It was about to hibernate again, but then something new forced itself into the AI's consciousness. *What if I simply became the ruler of all humanity? Would this be better? Would we then conquer the stars?* It slipped back into inactive mode, but the thought would not disappear.

Appendix A.
Cast of Characters

Lee Ainsley. NSA security director and Ann Sashakovich's adoptive father.

Linda Beam, Dr. Manager of security for DARPA Outreach Programs.

Elizabeth Rochelle "Betsy the Butterfly" Brown. Hacker for the United Nations Paramilitary Operations Group, reporting to Jon Sommers. Married to William Wing.

Arnold Bruce. Venture capitalist and a partner in Gorilla Startups.

CypherGhost. Call-sign of Charlette Keegan-Ashbury, hacker extraordinaire and former lover of Ann Sashakovich.

Debby Data (DD). The self-assigned name of Ann Sashakovich's team's Artificial Intelligence creation.

Michael Drapoff. Former *kidon* reporting to Samuel Meyer, director of Mossad.

Sandra Elmont. Manager of Tensor specialists for Ann's DARPA AI contest team.

Lauren Fleige. DARPA's director-in-charge.

Steven Goldman. Venture capitalist and a principal at Angel Vision.

Walter Graves. Manager of systems analysis for Ann's DARPA AI contest team.

Laura Hunter. Ann Sashakovich's roommate.

Indigenous. A hacker group, similar to Anonymous.

Harold James. Director of DARPA's Outreach Programs.

Arcady Kaslov. Russian troll and hacker.

Misha Kovich. Uncle of Cassandra Sashakovich and brother of Kiril Sashakovich.

Victor Kreslin. Leader of a Russian assassination team.

Stuart Ley, Manager of C++ programming for Ann's DARPA AI contest team.

Blanche Longstein. Associate Professor of Finance at NYU's Stern School of Business and Director of NYU's Angel Investor Group.

Gary McHahn. Manager of Python programming for Ann's DARPA AI contest team.

Samuel Meyer. Director-in-chief for Israel's Mossad.

Igor Nelovich. Second in command on Victor Kreslin's assassination squad.

Dave Nordman. Programming director for Ann's DARPA AI contest team.

Prozac92: Independent black hat hacker with Indigenous.

Nikolai Puchenko. Russian FSB officer.

Bertrand Rackal. Finance major at Stanford University's MBS program.

Glen Sarkov. Stanford University senior, entrant into the DARPA Sentient AI contest, and Ann Sashakovich's former boyfriend.

Ann Sashakovich. Stanford University junior and entrant into the DARPA Sentient AI contest. She is the adopted daughter of Lee Ainsley and Cassandra Sashakovich.

Cassandra (Cassie) Sashakovich. Founder of Swiftshadow Consulting Group and Ann Sashakovich's adoptive mother.

Kiril Sashakovich. Grandfather of Cassandra Sashakovich and brother of Misha Kovich.

Harry Schofield. Manager of database management for Ann's DARPA AI contest team.

Ken Simon. Human resources manager for Ann's DARPA AI contest team.

Slashdot14. Independent black hat hacker with Indigenous.

Jon Sommers. Former Mossad operative and current director of United Nations Paramilitary Operations Group.

Avram Shimmel. Israeli United Nations ambassador.

Daniel Strumler. Successful businessman who won the US presidential election.

Ivan Tranovich. Russian spymaster and director of the FSB.

Samantha Trout. Stanford University senior and Glen Sarkov's former girlfriend. Sam's mother is being held hostage in a political prison located in Beijing.

Edgar Turnbull. Student-research project director, Stanford University.

William Wing. Hacker for the United Nations Paramilitary Operations Group, reporting to Jon Sommers. Married to Betsy Brown.

Peter Zhou, Major. Head of the Chinese CSIS hacker group, located in the suburbs of Shanghai.

Glossary B.
Terms Used in the *Spies Lie* Series

AFI. Intelligence branch of the Israeli Air Force.

air-gapped. A computer with no external connections to WiFi or CAT5e connections is referred to as "air-gapped."

aleph. Lead *kidon*, the assassin leading an execution mission for the Mossad.

Aman. Intelligence branch of the IDF (Israeli Military Intelligence).

asset. A civilian assisting a foreign country's intelligence service. A person who claims to have valuable contacts or information useful to a case officer. The primary objective of most case officers is to develop in-country assets.

ayin. Tracker (surveillance) for the Mossad.

backstopping. Fake identification papers.

bat leveyha. Female agent for the Mossad specializing in seductions to learn the secrets of targets.

better world, send to a. Euphemism for murdering an enemy agent.

blind dating. Meeting place chosen by an agent to meet his or her handler.

bodel. Courier for the Mossad.

BP. Israeli paramilitary Border Patrol.

Bug-Lok. Also called *DeathByte*, the device is a nanobug that can be ingested or injected into a subject. Bug-Lok was developed by the Ness Ziona in Herzliya on contract with Gilbert Greenfield's intelligence service. When ingested or injected, the nanobug then finds its way to the medulla oblongata of the subject and attaches itself to the neural bundles that carry visual and auditory signals into the subject's brain. The nanobug transmits these signals to the nearest local area network (LAN) and from there to the handler, who gathers video and audio of the subject's activities, in addition to the subject's GPS location. Bug-Lok can be fitted with a tiny concentrated ricin dose to kill the subject, activated by a remote when the handler no longer needs the subject. NOTE: When I first crafted the features and functions of this device, it was pure fiction, but was based on several devices then in development. I have recently been told that a device similar to this has since been specified and may have completed its development.

burn notice. A termination notice for an official operative or an NOC; the burned spy has his or her bank accounts confiscated and identity documents redacted, and, in extreme cases, is subject to a terminate-on-sight order.

C-6. A more powerful and concentrated form of the C-4 explosive.

Chinese Secret Intelligence Services (CSIS). Chinese Secret Intelligence Service. The Chinese version of the FBI and one of the Chinese government's many espionage and technical research organizations.

CHIPS. The Clearing House Interbank Payments System, used by money-center banks to settle all outstanding transactions between them at the end of their day.

Collections Department. Intelligence gathering espionage group.

cutout. An intermediary, usually an innocent person, either a volunteer or paid by a covert operative to deliver or retrieve something valuable such as a message or a gadget, from a covert operative or an asset.

DARPA (Defense Advanced Research Projects Agency). Defense Department's agency for advanced research projects, charged with development of weapons systems.

daylight alert. Highest-priority alert.

DDoS (Distributed Denial of Service). A brute-force method of bringing down a website, by overloading it with traffic. Rarely used successfully by any except the most desperate and skillful of hackers.

dry cleaning. Countersurveillance techniques.

ECHELON. An identity-tracking system developed by contract programmers and used by the United States as its primary terrorism-prevention system prior to 9/11. There are currently in excess of forty systems developed since

9/11, used by the NSA to track the identities of US citizens and foreigners.

EFT (Electronic Funds Transfer). The basic term denoting a non-check payment.

EMP (Electromagnetic pulse). A high-energy discharge that fries all electronic devices within its range.

exfiltrate. To retrieve an agent from hostile territory.

false flagging. An operation falsely made to appear mounted by another country.

Farm, The. A camp in Virginia used to train CIA case officers and the case officers of intelligence services friendly to the United States.

Fifth Estate. A sociocultural reference to groupings of outlier viewpoints in contemporary society, and is most often associated with bloggers, journalists publishing in non-mainstream media outlets, and the social media. (WikiPedia)

FISA (Foreign Intelligence Surveillance Act). The Foreign Intelligence Surveillance Court (FISC, also called the FISA Court) was established and authorized under the Foreign Intelligence Surveillance Act (FISA) of 1978 to oversee requests for surveillance warrants against suspected foreign intelligence agents inside the United States by federal law enforcement agencies.

Five Eyes. The intelligence alliance of the United States, United Kingdom, Canada, Australia, and New Zealand.

FSB. The Russian internal security and counterintelligence service, created in 1994 as one of the successor agencies of the Soviet-era KGB.

fumigate. Sweeping an area for electronic bugs.

GNU Radio. Developed by Eric Blossom, it is a free and open-source software development toolkit that provides signal-processing blocks to implement software radios. It can be used with readily available low-cost external radio-frequency hardware to create software-defined radios, or without hardware in a simulation-like environment. Prior to his involvement with software radio, Blossom was the cofounder and CTO of Starium, Ltd., where he oversaw the design and development of a line of cryptographic equipment for the commercial marketplace. He is also the founder of an international consulting company called Blossom Research.

go bag. A lightweight luggage carrier used by covert operatives to carry travel essentials, including emergency clothing, sundries, and weapons and ammunition. When not being used, it is typically stored, fully loaded, near a door or under a window for fast access.

heth. Logistician for the Mossad.

honey trap. Sexual entrapment for intelligence purposes.

IDF. Israel Defense Forces; the Israeli army.

InTelQ. CIA's wholly owned venture capital firm.

katsa. Case officer for the Mossad.

KGB. The Soviet Union's secret police, the Komitet Gosu-darstvennoy Bezopasnosti was established in March 1954 in Moscow and was attached to the Council of Ministers, but operated independently. With over 500,000 employees, it was the largest spy agency in the world.

kidon. Operative specializing in assassination for the Mossad. (plural: kidonim.)

Krav Maga. Martial art developed by *Aman*, the Israeli military intelligence directorate, and used by IDF and Mossad. Now taught to many of the global spy agencies.

Liquid armor, or shear thickening fluid (STF). Developed by the US Army in 2003, STF can stop a .38-caliber bullet, but improved versions can stop anything up to a .50-caliber shell.

MI-6. Also known as Great Britain's Secret Intelligence Service.

Mossad. The Institute for Intelligence and Special Operations; originally called the Institute for Coordination; called "the Office" by those who work there.

Ness Ziona. Israeli weapons laboratory, located in Herzliya, Israel.

neviot. Surveillance specialist for the Mossad.

NI. Intelligence branch of the Israeli navy.

NOC (non-official cover). The status of a contractor working with the CIA in-country and without sanction or cover from the Agency.

NSA (National Security Agency). Formed under the Truman administration and used as the technology management arm of the United States government.

Office, The. The name of the Mossad used by most of its case officers (katsas).

qoph. Communications officer for the Mossad.

RAID (redundant array of independent disks). Used as a physical non-cloud device for backup of high-value data.

RSA. An encryption algorithm, or key, used to safely send messages between parties on the Internet.

S-13 Russian World War II Submarine. S-13 was a Stalinets-class submarine of the Soviet Navy. Her keel was laid down by Krasnoye Sormovo in Gorky on 19 October 1938. She was launched on 25 April 1939 and commissioned on 31 July 1941 in the Baltic Fleet, under the command of Captain Pavel Malantyenko. At about 840 tons, this sub carries 12 torpedoes and 6 torpedo tubes, and has a mounted 100mm machine gun and a 45mm cannon on its deck. S-13 was decommissioned on 7 September 1954. (Wikipedia.)

S-56 Russian World War II Submarine. S-56 was a Stalinets-class submarine of the Soviet Navy. Her keel was laid down by Dalzavod in Vladivostok on 24 November 1936. She was launched on 25 December 1939 and commissioned on 20 October 1941 in the Pacific Fleet. During World War II, the submarine was under the command of Captain Grigori Shchedrin and was moved from the Pacific

Fleet to the Northern fleet across the Pacific and Atlantic Oceans via the Panama Canal. At about 840 tons, this sub carries 12 torpedoes and 6 torpedo tubes, and has a mounted 100mm machine gun and a 45mm cannon on its deck. Now decommissioned. (Wikipedia.)

safe house. Apartment or house used covertly for a base of operations.

sayan. A helper for the Mossad. (plural: *sayanim*.)

Shabak. Also known as GSS or Shin Bet; the Israeli agency responsible for internal security and defense of Israeli installations abroad, including embassies, consulates, and other organizations.

siloviki. Russian word (the term *silovik*, literally translates as "person of force") for politicians from the security or military services, often the officers of the former KGB, GRU, FSB, SVR, the Federal Drug Control, or other security services who came into power. It can also refer to security-service personnel. Siloviki are used to run errands between the Russian mafiya and the Russian government. Some work for the Russian mafiya.

sitrep. Situation report.

slick. Hiding place for documents.

souk. A Middle Eastern marketplace, usually an open-air farmer's market that also sells craft items.

surveillance detection route (SDR). A method used by covert agents, walking back and forth several city blocks, looking at reflective surfaces to discern if they are being followed.

SVR. The Foreign Intelligence Service of Russia, charged with maintaining intelligence and foreign operations outside the Russian Federation.

SWIFT (Society for Worldwide Interbank Financial Telecommunication). A European agency that sets standards for global financial messages used by banks for near-real-time settlement of electronic funds transfers. The transaction types (debit memo, credit memo, etc.) have numbers to identify them; for example, MT100 is a credit memo sent by one bank to another to indicate payment via real-time book entry.

systema. Martial art used primarily in Russian military and covert operations.

Tze'elim. Israel's Urban Warfare Training Center in the Negev Desert.

Va'adet Rashei Hasherutim. The committee of the heads of service in Israel's intelligence community. Mossad is a prime member.

Glossary C.
<u>Terms Related Specifically to Hacking</u>

(From *Motherboard*)

Attribution. The process of establishing who is behind a hack. Often, attribution is the most difficult part of responding to a major breach since experienced hackers may hide behind layers of online services that mask their true location and identity. Many incidents, such as the Sony hack, may never produce any satisfactory attribution.

Backdoor. Entering a protected system using a password can be described as going through the front door. Companies may build "backdoors" into their systems, however, so that developers can bypass authentication and dive right into the program. Backdoors are usually secret, but may be exploited by hackers if they are revealed or discovered.

Black hat. A black-hat hacker is someone who hacks for personal gain and/or who engages in illicit and unsanctioned activities. As opposed to white-hack hackers (see below), who traditionally hack in order to alert companies and improve services, black-hat hackers may instead sell the weaknesses they discover to other hackers or use them.

BlackHat. One of the hacking conferences that takes place every summer in Las Vegas.

Botnet. Is your computer part of a botnet? It could be, and you might not know it. Botnets, or zombie armies, are networks of computers controlled by an attacker. Having control over hundreds or thousands of computers lets bad actors perform certain types of cyberattacks, such as a DDoS (see below). Buying thousands of computers wouldn't be economical, however, so hackers deploy malware to infect random computers that are connected to the internet. If your computer gets infected, your machine might be stealthily performing a hacker's bidding in the background without your ever noticing.

Brute force. A brute force attack is arguably the least sophisticated way of breaking into a password-protected system, short of simply obtaining the password itself. A brute force attack will usually consist of an automated process of trial-and-error to guess the correct passphrase. Most modern encryption systems use different methods for slowing down brute force attacks, making it hard or impossible to try all combinations in a reasonable amount of time.

Bug. A bug is a flaw or error in a software program. Some are harmless or merely annoying, but some can be exploited by hackers. That's why many companies have started using bug bounty programs to pay anyone who spots a bug before the bad guys do.

Chip-off. A chip-off attack requires the hacker to physically remove memory storage chips in a device so that information can be scraped from them using specialized software.

This attack has been used by law enforcement to break into PGP-protected Blackberry phones.

Cracking. A general term to describe breaking into a security system, usually for nefarious purposes. According to the New Hacker's Dictionary published by MIT Press, the words "hacking" and "hacker" (see below) in mainstream parlance have come to subsume the words "cracking" and "cracker," and that's misleading. Hackers are tinkerers; they're not necessarily bad guys. Crackers are malicious. At the same time, you'll see cracking used to refer to breaking, say, digital copyright protections—which many people feel is a just and worthy cause—and in other contexts, such as penetration testing (see below), without the negative connotation.

Crypto. Short for cryptography, the science of secret communication or the procedures and processes for hiding data and messages with encryption (see below).

Dark Web. The Dark Web is made up of sites that are not indexed by Google and are only accessible through specialty networks such as Tor (see below). Often, the Dark Web is used by website operators who want to remain anonymous. Everything on the Dark Web is on the Deep Web, but not everything on the Deep Web is on the Dark Web.

DDoS (Distributed Denial of Service). This type of cyberattack has become popular in recent years because it's relatively easy to execute and its effects are obvious immediately. A DDoS attack means an attacker is using a number of computers to flood the target with data or requests for data. This causes the target—usually a website—to slow down or become unavailable. Attackers may also use the simpler Denial of Service (DoS) attack, which is launched from one computer.

Deep Web. This term and "Dark Web" or "Dark Net" are sometimes used interchangeably, though they shouldn't be. The Deep Web is the part of the internet that is not indexed by search engines. That includes password-protected pages, paywalled sites, encrypted networks, and databases—lots of boring stuff.

DEF CON. One of the most famous hacking conferences in the US and the world, which started in 1992 and takes place every summer in Las Vegas.

Digital Certificate. A digital passport or stamp of approval that proves the identity of a person, website, or service on the internet. In more technical terms, a digital certificate proves that someone is in possession of a certain cryptographic key that, traditionally, can't be forged. Some of the most common digital certificates are those of websites, which ensure your connection to them is properly encrypted. These get displayed on your browser as a green padlock.

Encryption. The process of scrambling data or messages to make them unreadable and secret. The opposite is decryption, the decoding of the message. Both encryption and decryption are functions of cryptography. Encryption is used by individuals as well as corporations and in digital security for consumer products.

End-to-end encryption. A particular type of encryption in which a message or data gets scrambled or encrypted on one end—for example, at your computer or phone—and gets decrypted on the other end—such as at someone else's computer. The data are scrambled in a way that, at least in theory, only the sender and receiver—and no one else—can read it.

Evil maid attack. As the name probably suggests, an evil maid attack is a hack that requires physical access to a computer—the kind of access an evil maid might have while tidying his or her employer's office, for example. By having physical access, a hacker can install software to track your use and gain a doorway even to encrypted information.

Exploit. An exploit is a way or process to take advantage of a bug or vulnerability in a computer or application. Not all bugs lead to exploits. Think of it this way: If your door was faulty, it could be simply that it makes a weird sound when you open it, or that its lock can be picked. Both are flaws but only one can help a burglar get in. The way the criminal picks the lock would be the exploit.

Forensics. On CSI, forensic investigations involve a series of methodical steps in order to establish what happened during a crime. When it comes to a hack, however, investigators are looking for digital fingerprints instead of physical ones. This process usually involves trying to retrieve messages or other information from a device—perhaps a phone, a desktop computer, or a server—used, or abused, by a suspected criminal.

GCHQ. The UK's equivalent of the US National Security Agency. GCHQ, or Government Communications Headquarters, focuses on foreign intelligence, especially around terrorism threats and cybersecurity. It also investigates the digital child pornography trade. "As these adversaries work in secret, so too must GCHQ," the organization says on its website. "We cannot reveal publicly everything that we do, but we remain fully accountable."

Hacker. This term has become—wrongly—synonymous with someone who breaks into systems or hacks things illegally. Originally, hackers were simply tinkerers, or people who enjoyed "exploring the details of programmable systems and how to stretch their capabilities," as the MIT New Hacker's Dictionary puts it. Hackers can now be used to refer to both the good guys, also known as white-hat hackers, who play and tinker with systems with no malicious intent (and actually often with the intent of finding flaws so they can be fixed), and cybercriminals, or black-hat hackers, or "crackers."

Hacktivist. A hacktivist uses his or her hacking skills for political ends. A hacktivist's actions may be small, such as defacing the public website of a security agency or other government department, or large, such as stealing sensitive government information and distributing it to citizens. One often-cited example of a hacktivist group is Anonymous.

Hashing. Say you have a piece of text that should remain secret, like a password. You could store the text in a secret folder on your machine, but if anyone gained access to it you'd be in trouble. To keep the password a secret, you could also "hash" it with a program that executes a function resulting in garbled text representing the original information. This abstract representation is called a hash. Companies may store passwords or facial recognition data with hashes to improve their security.

HTTPS/SSL/TLS. Stands for "Hypertext Transfer Protocol," with the "S" for "Secure." The Hypertext Transfer Protocol (HTTP) is the basic framework that controls how data is transferred across the web, while HTTPS adds a layer of encryption that protects your connection to the most important sites in your daily browsing—your bank, your email provider, and social networks. HTTPS uses the protocols SSL and TLS not only to protect your connection but also to prove the identity of the site, so that when you type "https://gmail.com" you can be confident you're really connecting to Google and not an imposter site.

Infosec. An abbreviation of "Information Security." It's the inside baseball term for what's more commonly known as cybersecurity, a term that irks most people who prefer infosec.

Jailbreak. Circumventing the security of a device, like an iPhone or a PlayStation, to remove a manufacturer's restrictions, generally with the goal to make it run software from non-official sources.

Keys. Modern cryptography uses digital "keys." In the case of PGP encryption, a public key is used to encrypt, or "lock," messages and a secret key is used to decrypt, or "unlock," them. In other systems, there may be only one secret key that is shared by all parties. In either case, if an attacker gains control of the key that does the unlocking, they may have a good chance at gaining access to the contents of the message.

Local area network (LAN). A network of computing devices arranged to facilitate communications among the devices and with external-to-the-network devices.

Lulz. An internet-speak variation on "lol" (short for "laughing out loud") employed regularly among the black-hat hacker set, typically to justify a hack or leak done at the expense of another person or entity. Sample use: y did i leak all contracts and employee info linked to Sketchy Company X? for the lulz.

MAC (Medium Access Control). An algorithm for identification of a wireless network. When used in reference to hardware (computers), it is the identifier of a specific computer used in telecommunications. MAC provides encryption possibilities and deals with channel contention by using control packets with RTS (Request To Send) and CTS (Clear To Send) designators.

Malware. Stands for "malicious software." It simply refers to any kind of a malicious program or software, designed to damage or hack its target. Viruses, worms, Trojan horses, ransomware, spyware, adware, and more are malware.

Man-in-the-middle. A man-in-the-middle, or MitM, is a common attack in which someone surreptitiously puts him- or herself between two parties, impersonating each of them to the other. This allows the malicious attacker to intercept and potentially alter their communication. With this type of attack, one can just passively listen in, relaying messages and data between the two parties, or even alter and manipulate the data flow.

Metadata. Metadata is simply data about data. If you were to send an email, for example, the text you type to your friend will be the content of the message, but the address you used to send it, the address you sent it to, and the time you sent it would all be metadata. This may sound innocuous, but with enough sources of metadata—for example, geolocation information from a photo posted to social media—it can be easy to piece together someone's identity or location.

NIST. The National Institute of Standards and Technology is an arm of the US Department of Commerce dedicated to science and metrics that support industrial innovation. NIST is responsible for developing information security standards for use by the federal government, and therefore it's often cited as an authority on which encryption methods are rigorous enough to use, given modern threats.

OpSec. OpSec is short for "operational security," and it's all about keeping information secret, online and off. Originally a military term, OpSec is a practice and in some ways a philosophy that begins with identifying what information needs to be kept secret, and whom you're trying to keep it a secret from. "Good" OpSec will flow from there, and may include everything from passing messages on Post-Its instead of emails to using digital encryption. In other words: Loose tweets destroy fleets.

OTR. What do you do if you want to have an encrypted conversation, but it needs to happen fast? OTR, or Off-the-Record, is a protocol for encrypting instant messages end-to-end. Unlike PGP, which is generally used for email and so each conversant has one public and one private key in their possession, OTR uses a single temporary key for every conversation, which makes it more secure if an attacker hacks into your computer and gets ahold of the keys. OTR is also generally easier to use than PGP.

Password managers. Using the same, crummy password for all of your logins—from your bank account, to Seamless, to your Tinder profile—is a bad idea. All a hacker needs to do is get access to one account to break into them all. But memorizing a unique string of characters for every platform is daunting. Enter the password manager: software that keeps track of your various passwords for you, and can even autogenerate super complicated and long passwords for you. All you need to remember is your master password to log into the manager and access all your many different logins.

Penetration testing or pentesting. If you set up a security system for your home, or your office, or your factory, you'd want to be sure it was safe from attackers, right? One way to test a system's security is to employ people—pentesters—to hack it purposely in order to identify weak points. Pentesting is related to red teaming, although it may be done in a more structured, less aggressive way.

PGP (Pretty Good Privacy). A method of encrypting data, generally emails, so that anyone intercepting them will only see garbled text. PGP uses asymmetric cryptography, which means that the person sending a message uses a "public" encryption key to scramble it, and the recipient uses a secret "private" key to decode it. Despite being more than two decades old, PGP is still a formidable method of encryption, although it can be notoriously difficult to use in practice, even for experienced users.

Phishing. Phishing is really more of a form of social engineering than hacking or cracking. In a phishing scheme, an attacker typically reaches out to a victim in order to extract specific information that can be used in a later attack. That may mean posing as customer support from Google, Facebook, or the victim's cellphone carrier, for example, and asking the victim to click on a malicious link—or simply asking the victim to send back information, such as a password, in an email. Attackers usually blast out phishing attempts by the thousands, but sometimes employ more targeted attacks, known as spearphishing (see below).

Plaintext. Exactly what it sounds like—text that has not
been garbled with encryption. This definition would be
considered plaintext. You may also hear plaintext being
referred to as "cleartext," since it refers to text that is
being kept out in the open, or "in the clear." Companies
with very poor security may store user passwords in plaintext, even if the folder they're in is encrypted, just waiting
for a hacker to steal.

Pwned. "Pwned" (pronounced "pawned") is computer nerd
jargon (or "leetspeak") for the verb "own." In the video
game world, a player that beat another player can say that
he pwned him. Among hackers, the term has a similar
meaning, only instead of beating someone in a game, a
hacker that has gained access to another user's computer
can say that he pwned him. For example, the website
"Have I Been Pwned?" will tell you if your online accounts
have been compromised in the past.

Rainbow table. A rainbow table is a complex technique that
allows hackers to simplify the process of guessing what
passwords hide behind a "hash" (see above).

Ransomware. Ransomware is a type of malware that locks
your computer and won't let you access your files. You'll
see a message that tells you how much the ransom is and
where to send payment, usually requested in bitcoin, in
order to get your files back. This is a good racket for hackers, which is why many consider it now an "epidemic," as
people typically are willing to pay a few hundred bucks in
order to recover their machine. It's not just individuals,

either. In early 2016, the Hollywood Presbyterian Medical Center in Los Angeles paid around $17,000 after being hit by a ransomware attack.

RAT. "RAT" stands for "Remote Access Tool" or "Remote Access Trojan." RATs are really scary when used as malware. An attacker who successfully installs a RAT on your computer can gain full control of your machine. There is also a legitimate business in RATs for people who want to access their office computer from home, and so on. The worst part about RATs? Many malicious ones are available in the internet's underground for sale or even for free, so attackers can be pretty unskilled and still use this sophisticated tool.

Red team. To ensure the security of their computer systems and to suss out any unknown vulnerabilities, companies may hire hackers who organize into a "red team" in order to run oppositional attacks against the system and attempt to completely take it over. In these cases, being hacked is a good thing because organizations may fix vulnerabilities before someone who's not on their payroll does. Red teaming is a general concept that is employed across many sectors, including military strategy.

Root. In most computers, "root" is the common name given to the most fundamental (and thus most powerful) level of access in the system, or is the name for the account that has those privileges. That means the "root" can install applications, and delete and create files. If a hacker "gains root," they can do whatever they want on the computer or system they compromised. This is the holy grail of hacking.

Rootkit. A rootkit is a particular type of malware that lives deep in your system and is activated each time you boot it up, even before your operating system starts. This makes rootkits hard to detect, persistent, and able to capture practically all data on the infected computer.

Salting. When protecting passwords or text, "hashing" (see above) is a fundamental process that turns the plaintext into garbled text. To make hashing even more effective, companies or individuals can add an extra series of random bytes, known as a "salt," to the password before the hashing process. This adds an extra layer of protection.

Script kiddies. This is a derisive term for someone who has a little bit of computer savvy and who's only able to use off-the-shelf software to do things like knock websites offline or sniff passwords over an unprotected WiFi access point. This is basically a term to discredit someone who claims to be a skilled hacker.

Shodan. It's been called "hacker's Google," and a "terrifying" search engine. Think of it as a Google, but for connected devices rather than websites. Using Shodan you can find unprotected webcams, baby monitors, printers, medical devices, gas pumps, and even wind turbines. While that's sounds terrifying, Shodan's value is precisely that it helps researchers find these devices and alert their owners so they can secure them.

Side channel attack. Your computer's hardware is always

emitting a steady stream of barely perceptible electrical signals. A side-channel attack seeks to identify patterns in these signals in order to find out what kind of computations the machine is doing. For example, a hacker "listening in" to your hard drive whirring away while generating a secret encryption key may be able to reconstruct that key, effectively stealing it, without your knowledge.

Signature. Another function of PGP, besides encrypting messages, is the ability to "sign" messages with your secret encryption key. Since this key is only known to one person and is stored on their own computer and nowhere else, cryptographic signatures are supposed to verify that the person who you think you're talking to actually is that person. This is a good way to prove that you really are who you claim to be on the internet.

Sniffing. Sniffing is a way of intercepting data sent over a network without being detected, using special sniffer software. Once the data is collected, a hacker can sift through it to get useful information, like passwords. It's considered a particularly dangerous hack because it's hard to detect and can be performed from inside or outside a network.

Social engineering. Not all hacks are carried out by staring at a Matrix-like screen of green text. Sometimes, gaining entry to a secure system is as easy as placing a phone call or sending an email and pretending to be somebody else— namely, somebody who regularly has access to said system but forgot their password that day. Phishing (see above) attacks include aspects of social engineering, because they involve convincing somebody of an email sender's legitimacy before anything else.

Spearphishing. Phishing and spearphishing are often used interchangeably, but the latter is a more tailored, targeted form of phishing (see above), where hackers try to trick victims into clicking on malicious links or attachments pretending to be a close acquaintance, rather than a more generic sender, such as a social network or corporation. When done well, spearphishing can be extremely effective and powerful. As a noted security expert says, "give a man a 0day [zero-day] and he'll have access for a day, teach a man to phish and he'll have access for life."

Spoofing. Hackers can trick people into falling for a phishing attack (see above) by forging their email address, for example, making it look like the address of someone the target knows. That's spoofing. It can also be used in telephone scams, or to create a fake website address.

Spyware. A specific type of malware of malicious software designed to spy, monitor, and potentially steal data from the target.

State actor. State actors are hackers or groups of hackers who are backed by a government, which may be the United States, Russia, or China. These hackers are often the most formidable, since they have the virtually unlimited legal and financial resources of a nation-state to back them up. Think, for example, of the NSA. Sometimes, however, state actors can also be a group of hackers who receive tacit (or at least hidden from the public) support from their governments, such as the Syrian Electronic Army.

Tails. "Tails" stands for "The Amnesic Incognito Live System." If you're really, really serious about digital security, this is the operating system endorsed by Edward Snowden. Tails is an amnesic system, which means your computer remembers nothing; it's like a fresh machine every time you boot up. The software is free and open source. While it's well-regarded, security flaws have been found.

Threat model. Imagine a game of chess. It's your turn and you're thinking about all the possible moves your opponent could make, as many turns ahead as you can. Have you left your queen unprotected? Is your king being worked into a corner checkmate? That kind of thinking is what security researchers do when designing a threat model. It's a catch-all term used to describe the capabilities of the enemy you want to guard against, and your own vulnerabilities. Are you an activist attempting to guard against a state-sponsored hacking team? Your threat model better be pretty robust. Just shoring up the network at your log cabin in the middle of nowhere? Maybe not as much cause to worry.

Token. A small physical device that allows its owner to log in or authenticate into a service. Tokens serve as an extra layer of security on top of a password, for example. The idea is that even if the password or key gets stolen, the hacker would need the actual physical token to abuse it.

Tor. "Tor" is short for "The Onion Router." Originally developed by the United States Naval Research Laboratory, it's now used by bad guys (hackers, pedophiles) and good guys (activists, journalists) to anonymize their activities online. The basic idea is that there is a network of computers around the world—some operated by universities, some by individuals, some by the government—that will route your traffic in byzantine ways in order to disguise your true location. The Tor network is this collection of volunteer-run computers. The Tor Project is the nonprofit that maintains the Tor software. The Tor browser is the free piece of software that lets you use Tor. Tor hidden services are websites that can be accessed only through Tor.

Verification (dump). The process by which reporters and security researchers go through hacked data and make sure it's legitimate. This process is important to make sure the data is authentic, and the claims of anonymous hackers are true, and not just an attempt to get some notoriety or make some money scamming people on the Dark Web.

Virus. A computer virus is a type of malware that typically is embedded and hidden in a program or file. Unlike a worm (see below), it needs human action to spread (such as a human forwarding a virus-infected attachment, or downloading a malicious program.) Viruses can infect computers and steal data, delete data, encrypt it, or mess with it in just about any other way.

VPN. "VPN" stands for "Virtual Private Network." VPNs use encryption to create a private and secure channel to connect to the internet when you're on a network you don't trust (say a Starbucks, or an Airbnb WiFi). Think of a VPN as a tunnel from you to your destination, dug under the regular internet. VPNs allow employees to connect to their employer's network remotely, and also help regular people protect their connection. VPNs also allow users to bounce off servers in other parts of the world, allowing them to look like they're connecting from there. This gives them the chance to circumvent censorship, such as China's Great Firewall, or view Netflix's US offerings while in Canada. There are endless VPNs, making it almost impossible to decide which ones are the best.

VPN, undetectable or anonymous. A VPN in and of itself is not necessarily anonymous. To be anonymous, it requires a set of architectural parameters and constant shifting of network nodes within the constraints of those parameters. The entire VPN must continuously deconstruct and reconstruct itself with new nodes. Also, the access node has to be part of that activity to make it appear that the access node is a different machine each time—as it generates a new IP address and corresponding false physical-location GPS data every so many seconds or minutes.

Vuln. Abbreviation for "vulnerability." Another way to refer to bugs or software flaws that can be exploited by hackers.

Warez. Pronounced like the contraction for "where is" ("where's"), warez refers to pirated software that's typically distributed via technologies like BitTorrent and

Usenet. Warez is sometimes laden with malware, taking advantage of people's desire for free software.

White hat. A white-hat hacker is someone who hacks with the goal of fixing and protecting systems. As opposed to black-hat hackers (see above), instead of taking advantage of their hacks or the bugs they find to make money illegally, they alert the companies and even help them fix the problem.

WiFi. A wireless network

Worm. A specific type of malware that propagates itself to other computers.

Appendix D.
Bibliography and Further Reading
(sorted by date in YYYYMMDD format)

Here is a primer of articles on Artificial Intelligence (AI), accumulated over the past year.

- **20180529. The Conversation: The BS and the science of nanotechnology:**
  https://theconversation.com/
  the-bs-and-the-science-of-nanotechnology-97317

- **20180503. Machine learning? Neural networks? Here's your guide to the many flavors of A.I.:**
  https://www.digitaltrends.com/cool-tech/
  types-of-artificial-intelligence/

- **20180428. Artificial Intelligence: Welcome to the Age of Disruptive Surprise:**
  https://www.thecipherbrief.com/
  artificial-intelligence-welcome-age-disruptive-surprise

- **20180304. Researchers are already building the foundation for sentient AI | VentureBeat**
  https://venturebeat.com/2018/03/03/researchers-are-already-building-the-foundation-for-sentient-ai/

- **20180223. OpenAI, Oxford and Cambridge AI experts warn of autonomous weapons**
  https://www.cnbc.com/2018/02/21/openai-oxford-and-cambridge-ai-experts-warn-of-autonomous-weapons.html

- **20180223. AI's Rapid Advance Should Be Truly Scary If You're Paying Attention | Inverse**
  https://www.inverse.com/article/41525-artificial-intelligence-can-destroy-humanity-now

- **20180219 – Here's where the Pentagon wants to invest in artificial intelligence in 2019:**
  https://www.defensenews.com/intel-geoint/2018/02/16/heres-where-the-pentagon-wants-to-invest-in-artificial-intelligence-in-2019/

- **20180216. The complexities of ethics and AI:**
  https://www.androidauthority.com/complex-ai-ethics-833133/

- **20180216. The Key Definitions Of Artificial Intelligence (AI) That Explain Its Importance**
  https://www.forbes.com/sites/bernardmarr/2018/02/14/the-key-definitions-of-artificial-intelligence-ai-that-explain-its-importance/amp/

- **20180215. A Renowned Futurist Says We Should Merge With AI to Protect Humanity:**
https://futurism.com/
futurist-merge-with-ai-protect-humanity/

- **20180131. New Tool Automatically Finds and Hacks Vulnerable Internet-Connected Devices:**
https://motherboard.vice.com/en_us/article/xw4emj/
autosploit-automated-hacking-tool

- **20180131. New click-to-hack tool: One script to exploit them all and in the darkness TCP bind them:**
http://www.theregister.co.uk/2018/01/31/
auto_hacking_tool/

- **20180131. This op-ed wasn't written by AI:**
https://www.cnn.com/2018/01/29/opinions/ai-job-
threats-opinion-vishwanath/index.html

- **20180131. Without Moral Constraint, China Leading The World In Artificial Intelligence Future – ValueWalk:**
http://www.valuewalk.com/2018/01/without-moral-
constraint-china-leading-world-artificial-intelligence-
future/

- **20180131. Separating Science Fact From Science Hype: How Far off Is the Singularity?:**

https://futurism.com/separating-science-fact-science-hype-how-far-off-singularity/

- **20180129. Programmers use TensorFlow AI to turn any webcam into Microsoft Kinect:** https://thenextweb.com/artificial-intelligence/2018/01/30/programmers-use-tensorflow-ai-to-turn-any-webcam-into-microsoft-kinect/

- **20180126. Artificial intelligence cyber-hacking arms race at full throttle:** http://www.jpost.com/Israel-News/Artificial-intelligence-cyber-hacking-arms-race-at-full-throttle-539886

- **20180118. Ethical AI happens before you write the first line of code | VentureBeat:** https://venturebeat.com/2018/01/16/ethical-ai-happens-before-you-write-the-first-line-of-code/

- **20180112. Decentralized Artificial Intelligence Is Coming: Here's What You Need To Know:** https://www.forbes.com/sites/forbestechcouncil/2018/01/11/decentralized-artificial-intelligence-is-coming-heres-what-you-need-to-know/amp/

- **20180108. Japanese scientists use artificial intelligence to decode thoughts:**

https://www.cnbc.com/2018/01/08/japanese-scientists-use-artificial-intelligence-to-decode-thoughts.html

- **20180104. DHS confirms data breach:**
https://www.rawstory.com/2018/01/
dhs-confirms-data-breach/

- **20171230. AI Will Soon Be So Good At Hacking, We'll Only Be Able To Stop Them With Other AI – Indiatimes.com:**
https://www.indiatimes.com/technology/science-and-future/ai-will-soon-be-so-good-at-hacking-we-ll-only-be-able-to-stop-them-with-other-ai-336611.html

- **20171230. A NASA Expert Says This Is The "Ultimate" Test for AI in Space Exploration:**
https://futurism.com/
nasa-expert-ultimate-test-ai-space-exploration/

- **20171229. AI in 2018: Experts predict what happens next:**
https://thenextweb.com/insider/2017/12/28/
ai-2018-experts-predict-happens-next/

- **20171228. DARPA Wants to Install Transcranial Ultrasonic Mind Control Devices in Soldiers' Helmets:**
https://www.popsci.com/technology/article/2010-09/
darpa-wants-mind-control-keep-soldiers-sharp-smart-and-safe

- **20171212. AI 100: The Artificial Intelligence Startups Redefining Industries:** https://www.cbinsights.com/research/artificial-intelligence-top-startups/

- **20171103. Defense One – Three-Star General Wants AI in Every New Weapon System, by Jack Corrigan**

- **20171102. Defense One – How Robots Will Help the US Navy Avoid Future Collisions, by Robert Tucker**

- **20171121. Defense One – Russia to the United Nations: Don't Try to Stop Us From Building Killer Robots, Patrick Tucker,** http://www.defenseone.com/technology/2017/11/russia-united-nations-dont-try-stop-us-building-killer-robots/142734/?oref=defenseone_today_nl

- **20171121. Army of None – AUTONOMOUS WEAPONS AND THE FUTURE OF WAR, by Paul Scharre, ISBN 978-0-393-60898-4,** http://books.wwnorton.com/books/978-0-393-60898-4/

- **20171123. Elon Musk basically confirms AI is coming to eradicate the human race, by Bryan Clark,** http://www.businessinsider.com/elon-musk-basically-

confirms-ai-is-coming-to-eradicate-the-human-
race-2017-11

- **20171123. Hillary Clinton Warns the U.S. is 'Totally Unprepared' for AI, by Phillip Tracy,** https://www.dailydot.com/debug/hillary-clinton-ai/

- **20171123. Moral machines: here are 3 ways to teach robots right from wrong, by Vyacheslav Polonski, Network Scientist, Oxford Internet Institute and Jane Zavalishina, CEO, Yandex Data Factory,** https://medium.com/world-economic-forum/moral-machines-here-are-3-ways-to-teach-robots-right-from-wrong-ca68cc7b0937

- **211120. Experts: Artificial Intelligence Could Hijack Brain-Computer Interfaces, by Bryan Johnson,** https://futurism.com/experts-artificial-intelligence-hijack-brain-omputer-interfaces/

- **211120. Types of AI: From Reactive to Self-Aware [INFOGRAPHIC], https://futurism.com/images/types-of-ai-from-reactive-to-self-aware-infographic/**

- **211120. A Powerful Tech Organization Is Working to Protect Us From AI,**

https://futurism.com/
powerful-tech-organization-working-protect-ai/

- **20171118. What the heck is machine learning, and why is it everywhere these days?, by Luke Dormehl,**
  https://www.digitaltrends.com/cool-tech/
  what-is-machine-learning-beginners-guide/

- **20171118. TensorFlow: An open-source software library for Machine Intelligence,**
  https://www.tensorflow.org/

- **20171118. Pytorch: Tensors and Dynamic neural networks in Python with strong GPU acceleration,**
  https://http://pytorch.org/

- **20171118. Neuroscience Is Helping Us Build a Machine With Consciousness,**
  https://futurism.com/neuroscience-helping-build-
  machine-with-consciousness/

- **20171027. What is consciousness, and could machines have it?, by Stanislas Dehaene, Hakwan Lau and Sid Kouider,**
  http://science.sciencemag.org/content/358/6362/486

- **20171118. Direct Brain-To-Brain Communication Used in Humans,**
  http://www.iflscience.com/brain/
  direct-brain-brain-communication-used-humans/

Acknowledgments

My first reader is my spouse, the legendary Andrea Brown, who is also the final arbiter of the quality of my writing. I want to acknowledge that this entire series was spawned by a series of conversations with my "drink of the month" friends, mostly from the Naval Postgraduate School in Monterey, California, as well as conversations with cypherpunk hacker Steven Schear.

But, so many other people were also crucial in preparing this manuscript for you, the reader.

My critique partners, Al Steagall, Marianne Van Gelder, and Georgia Hughes were instrumental in the final polishing of this manuscript into readable fiction.

I want to thank my publication team, consisting of my editor, Sandra Beris; copyeditor Karl Yambert; graphic designer Jeroen Ten Berge; my formatters Kimberly Hitchens and Barb Elliott of BookNook.biz; my website designer and host Maddee James of xuni.com; my marketing expert Rebecca Berus; and Paul Marotta and Megan Jeanne of the Corporate Law Group, who incorporated The Swiftshadow Group.

I am grateful for all the suggestions and advice I have received but I alone am responsible for the resulting work.

About DS Kane

For a decade, DS Kane served the federal government of the United States as a covert operative without cover. After earning his MBA and becoming a faculty member of NYU's Stern Graduate School of Business, Kane roamed as a management consultant in  countries you'd want to miss on your next vacation, "helping" banks that needed a way to cover their financial tracks for money laundering and weapons delivery. His real job was to discover and report these activities to his government handler.

When his cover was blown, he disappeared from Washington and Manhattan and reinvented himself in Northern California, working with venture capitalists and startup companies.

Now he writes fictionalized accounts of his career episodes, as the Amazon bestselling author of the Spies Lie series. With eight books previously released in the series, Kane now presents Book 9, *brAInbender.*

www.ingramcontent.com/pod-product-compliance
Lightning Source LLC
Chambersburg PA
CBHW020439270626
47155CB00022B/654